Praise for The Falcon Club Series

THE ROGUE

"A strong and independent female protagonist."
Library Journal (starred review)

"The chemistry between them is electric ... Ashe's writing is lyrical and almost poetic in places ... and Saint is easily one of the finest romantic heroes I've read in quite some time."
All About Romance (Desert Island Keeper)

"The desperate yearning—and dangerous secrets—between the star-crossed lovers had my stomach in knots until the very end of this hypnotic book."
Amazon's Omnivorous (Best Romances of the Month)

"Powerful, suspenseful and sensual."
RT Book Reviews (TOP PICK!)

HOW A LADY WEDS A ROGUE

Recommended Read!
Woman's World Magazine

"Emotionally touching and sexually taut."
Kirkus Reviews

HOW TO BE A PROPER LADY

Ten Best Romances of 2012
Amazon Editors' Choice

"Everything fans of historical romance could want in a book."
Joyfully Reviewed

WHEN A SCOT LOVES A LADY

"Lushly intense romance . . . radiant prose."
Library Journal (starred review)

"Sensationally intelligent writing, and a true, weak-in-the-knees love story."
Barnes & Noble "Heart to Heart" Recommended Read!

HOW TO MARRY A HIGHLANDER

RITA® Award Finalist 2014
Romance Writers of America

Praise for The Prince Catchers Series

I LOVED A ROGUE

"Passionate, heart-wrenching, and thoroughly satisfying."
All About Romance (Desert Island Keeper)

"Katharine Ashe's historical romances are rich and inventive, unexpected and smart, and she doesn't pull any emotional punches. She writes with a wry, provocative, angst-y energy that compels you to keep turning pages, even when it means the thrill of a blissful read will be far too soon behind you."
USA Today, Must-Read Romance of 2015

I ADORED A LORD

"A riotous good time... Delicious."
Publishers Weekly

"In the vein of the British country house mysteries of the golden age of that genre when authors such as Agatha Christie, Dorothy B. Sayers, Georgette Heyer, and Margery Allingham were turning out classic tales... Ashe's novel is a worthy successor. ... If you like your romance with a shade of difference, a generous serving of mystery, and a blend of tenderness and sizzle, I highly recommend *I Adored a Lord*."
The Romance Dish (5 stars)

I MARRIED THE DUKE

Billet-Doux Books

THE SCOUNDREL & I

Katharine Ashe is the *USA Today* bestselling and award-winning author of romances that reviewers call "intensely lush" and "sensationally intelligent," including *My Lady, My Lord* and *How to Marry a Highlander*, finalists for the RITA® Award of the Romance Writers of America, and *How To Be a Proper Lady*, an Amazon Top Ten Romance of the Year. Her books are recommended by *Publishers Weekly, Woman's World* Magazine, *Booklist, Library Journal, USA Today*, Kirkus Reviews, Barnes & Noble, Amazon, and many others, and translated into languages across the world.

Also by Katharine Ashe

Falcon Club Series
The Earl
The Rogue
How a Lady Weds a Rogue
How to Be a Proper Lady
When a Scot Loves a Lady

Prince Catchers Series
I Loved a Rogue
I Adored a Lord
I Married the Duke

Rogues of the Sea Series
In the Arms of a Marquess
Captured by a Rogue Lord
Swept Away by a Kiss

Twist Series
My Lady, My Lord
Again, My Lord

Captive Bride (A Regency Ghost Novel)

Novellas
Kisses, She Wrote
How to Marry a Highlander
A Lady's Wish
How Angela Got Her Rogue Back (in *At the Duke's Wedding*)
The Day It Rained Books (in *At the Billionaire's Wedding*)

THE
SCOUNDREL
& I

THE SCOUNDREL & I: Copyright © 2016 Katharine Brophy Dubois.
Cover design © Carrie Divine/Seductive Designs.
Image © Novelstock
Image © Nongkran_ch (Nongkran Pornmingmas)/Depositphotos.com
ISBN 9780991641253 (Paperback)
Published by Billet-Doux Books.

To the Princesses ~

Every author should be so blessed.

With all of my love.

Chapter One

Summer 1821
Brittle & Sons, Printers
London

Sometimes an honest, affectionate girl is born into misfortune but, by the grace of God or Luck or Fate, eventually finds her way out of those sorry circumstances to live happily ever after. Gabrielle Flood was not, unfortunately, one of those girls. Which was the reason that at the age of twenty-six, despite a heart inclined to optimism and a character inclined to hard work, Elle decided once and for all there was no God in heaven, and no Luck but bad luck. As for Fate, *if* it existed, it was only the sort with one grotesque eyeball shared by three old crones and a pair of sharp, cutting shears, as she had read about in a book of ancient mythology: the merciless sort.

And so, as summertime shadows lengthened across the press room of Brittle & Sons, Printers, Elle committed her first crime ever.

Not *crime*, really. Not precisely. Rather, *misdeed*. She was only borrowing the printing type, not stealing it.

Of course if despicable, vindictive Jo Junior discovered it, he would claim she had stolen it, even if Mr. Brittle Senior and Charlie believed her story. But she and Charlie had been on the outs since she had asked his father to increase her weekly wages—unsuccessfully. Poor Charlie, he was as timid as a church mouse.

Josiah Brittle Junior was another sort of man altogether. He would have her thrown in prison for this.

But he would never learn of it. The Brittle family had gone to Bristol on holiday for a fortnight. Declaring a holiday for the clerk and pressmen as well, Mr. Brittle had left Elle to work alone. The shop was essentially closed, after all; they never allowed her to carry on business in their absence. "Girls don't have the head for it, Gabby," Jo Junior always said with a smirk. She would not have another chance like this until Christmas. And time had abruptly become of the essence.

Unlocking the wedges and quoins that held the hundreds of pieces of type tightly together in the frame, she hefted the chase from the press. It was not an entire broadsheet; she could not possibly carry a chase of that size the three blocks to her flat. It was only the text portion of Lady Justice's latest pamphlet, and this one happened to be brief. The remainder of the sheet would be advertisements. Setting down the heavy frame on a square of felt, she wrapped it carefully and tucked the edges of the felt into firm corners. At home, her grandmother would open the cloth, touch the type, and her face would shine.

It was all Elle could do for her now.

Each evening after the shops on Gracechurch Street closed, the byway swiftly emptied of traffic except for patrons of the King's Barrel. Elle's friends who worked at other shops had already gone home. Like Jo Junior, they would not understand her actions now. No one but Gram would.

Taking up her swaddled treasure, she locked the shop door behind her and started toward home. Keeping close to the buildings and making every step with great care, she passed into the alleyway that led to another alley, and then to her building.

When the horse barreled around the corner, Elle had the fleeting thought that she should have heard it coming.

Flinging herself backward as a scream tore from her throat, she flattened against the wall, slammed her elbow into a protruding brick, and dropped her bundle.

Dropped.

Hurled.

Flung.

She saw it all as though it were happening in a nightmare.

The corners of the felt tore loose, the fabric fluttered open, the chase struck the cobbles, snapped, and broke, and hundreds of little pieces of iron cascaded across the alleyway. Blinking into the dusk in shock and horror, she saw the grate of a drain not a yard away. A piece of type teetered on one metal slat.

"No," she whispered. "*No.*"

She could not move. Could not say another word. Could not make muscles function in her body or coherent thoughts form in her mind.

Heavy hooves clattered on the cobblestones. They came closer. Then closer. Then the horse was before her, a huge, dark beast clomping all over Brittle & Son's best broadsheet type.

"No!" she cried, her lungs stuck to her spine. "No! Oh, *no!*"

"You there," boomed a voice above the clomping. "Are you injured?" Clear, strong, and utterly confident, the voice did not ask. It commanded.

It shocked her out of paralysis.

Her gaze slid up—up the horse's powerful legs, up a shining black boot, up a thigh clad in breeches that defined hard muscles, up a broad chest encased in an exceedingly fine coat, up a sparkling white cravat that caught the remnants of evening light—to a face suffused with arrogance.

Nothing came to her tongue. Nothing to her lips. Nothing even in her throat. Type glinted dully against the gray cobbles, her life in ruin beneath a horse's giant shod hooves. And she could only stare mutely at its rider.

He had strong features, a straight-ish nose, a knick of a scar on his jaw, and raven hair curling beneath a silk hat. Clearly an aristocrat, and handsome as could be.

Elle did not care for aristocrats or handsomeness. She had learned the hard way that a man's fortune and outer appearance meant nothing; only his character mattered.

"Speak, quickly," he demanded. "Are you injured?" His eyes were vibrant blue, rimmed with pitch-black lashes, and brimming with impatience. *Impatience.* As though *she* had

inconvenienced *him* by getting knocked aside by *his* horse.
Sickness crawled up her throat. To be ruined by this—*this*
sort of man—it was too horrible.
She could not speak. She shook her head.
With a last penetrating stare, he wheeled his giant mount
about and spurred it away. The clattering hooves faded, the
street again fell into quiet, and Elle stood amidst her ruination
and could not summon even a single sob.

~o0o~

Elle opened the door to her flat with the key hidden under
the mat that allowed the grocer's boy to deliver food and the
kind young curate from the charity church to visit. It was a
poor hiding place, but she and her grandmother had nothing
to steal anyway.
Filling her nose with air scented by the tea and toast that
she had made for her grandmother before departing for work
that morning, she laid an apron on the table and ladled type
onto it from her pockets. Gram had not left her bedchamber
in nearly two months. She would not discover this evidence of
Elle's foolishness, this disaster that would lead to her
termination at Brittle & Sons. Gram would have no reason to
worry.
Swiftly she prepared a bowl of porridge and a pot of tea,
then carried them in to the bedchamber.
Wrapped in shawls, with a cap over her gray curls, her
grandmother slept in the rocking chair. When Elle's foot
depressed the creaking board at the doorway, Gram's eyes
opened and a smile stirred her lips.
"Reverend Curtis must have visited today. You are
wearing your Sunday shawl." Elle set down the tray. "How did
he find you?"
"Dancing . . . on the table," her grandmother rasped, but
the shadow of a smile remained. "Have you brought it?"
"As promised, her latest!" Elle reached into her pocket
and withdrew a folded sheet of paper. "Charlie made the print

before he left for Bristol this morning, so that I can correct it while they are gone." Unfolding the sheet with a crinkle, she opened it across her lap. "But first you must eat."

"Mr. Curtis brought a meat pie."

"A meat pie?" Impossible. She'd taken no more than porridge and toast for weeks.

With a tiny jerk of her chin, Gram gestured to the broadsheet on Elle's knees.

"All right. But after I read, you will eat this porridge." But she knew Gram would not eat it. It would instead become her own dinner, if she could force it into her sick stomach. She smoothed out the creases of the next publication of England's most popular and controversial pamphleteer, Lady Justice.

A reformist in the style of revolutionary Frenchwomen of a generation earlier, Lady Justice wrote scathing condemnations of everything worth condemning in Britain: elitist snobbery, wastes of government funds, inhumane labor conditions, the suffering of war veterans and orphans, and anything else that required fixing in England. Elle proof-corrected the pages of Lady Justice's pamphlets that Brittle & Sons published, then secretly carried home the discarded prints and read them aloud to her grandmother. Gram said Lady Justice's spirit reminded her of America, her home for thirty years, and got misty-eyed with happy remembrance.

But mostly Elle and her grandmother enjoyed Lady Justice's passionate public correspondence with "Peregrine," the head of a highly elite gentleman's club that Lady Justice had vowed to destroy.

"The nemeses are full of scorn for each other this week, as always," Elle said, then read aloud.

Fellow Citizens of Britain,
   See how the Head Bird Man imagines he is diving for the kill, while his attack amounts to a mere fluffing of feathers. I offer to you his latest letter to me here in full. (As we have long known, he is as Eloquent as he is Wise, Good, and Useful to Society, which is to say

not at all.)

Dearest Lady,
    In your latest screed you call for Parliament to ensure women's rights, yet you are going about it all wrong. In the time-honored tradition of the feminine sex, you would be more likely to succeed in obtaining your desires if you flirted, cajoled, and petted. Instead you complain, insult, and demand. A man likes above all else a sweet tongue and a soft caress. Offer those and half the men in Government will be yours for the taking.

In guarded admiration,
Peregrine
Secretary, The Falcon Club

Fellow Citizens, if by "complain" he means that I make plain the inequities between men and women, and between rich and poor in this society; if by "insult" he means that I reveal the gross imbalance of power; and if by "demand" he means that I cry out for justice, he is speaking with more Sound Truth than ever before. Alas, he does not mean any of that. Full of masculine conceit, in order to coax me into softness he employs the very tactics he attributes to women: flirtation, cajolery, and caresses. In recommending that I behave with greater attention to my femininity, he himself practices feminine wiles.
    I will not be enticed.
    Mr. Peregrine, beware. For someday women will enjoy equal rights to men. On that day your arrogance will be stripped naked, your flatteries bared, and you will be forced to meet me eye to eye. When that day comes, pray that you remember how to be a Man.
                                                    — Lady Justice

    Her grandmother's eyes were twinkling brighter than they had in weeks.
    "Sweet tongue and . . ." Gram drew a rattling breath. "Soft caress?"

"Yours for the taking?" Elle said.

"Stripped . . . naked?"

"And *bared.* Can you believe it?" Elle clapped her hands onto the page. "Oh, Gram, they are positively besotted with each other!"

"How wonderful it is . . . to hear you laugh, Gabrielle. I feared . . . that I might never hear that sound again."

Elle dropped the pamphlet and grasped her grandmother's fragile hand.

"You mustn't say that, dear. You will be well soon enough."

"I worry . . ." Her grandmother's shallow breath did not even stir the coverlet over her chest. "That you will be alone."

"I am not alone. I have you. And Mineola and Adela and Esme, of course."

"You have closed off your heart," her grandmother whispered. Her energy was already gone, even after so few minutes awake, and Elle's heart did not feel closed off at all. It hurt beyond endurance. "Your mother . . . would not have wanted this."

"My mother's heart was far too open to men of poor character." And Elle had followed naïvely in those footsteps. Now she knew better.

Her grandmother gave no response.

Elle sat with her until she slept deeply, the pleasure she had taken in Lady Justice and Peregrine's latest brawl slipping swiftly away. The curate, Mr. Curtis, had confirmed her fears: her grandmother's remaining days were few. And the gift she longed to give her—to run her frail fingertips across the type, to feel the words and pluck out the mistakes as she had done in the governor of Virginia's workshop for years—was not to be. Tears welled in Elle's throat, but her eyes remained dry. She never wept. Ever. Not when her mother died, or her grandfather, or when horrid Jo Junior had played her for a fool and broken her heart.

Panic crawled up the back of her neck. She would not despair now, nor weep. Instead, tomorrow before the shops opened she would return to the alley and search until she found every last piece of type. Then she would repair the chase, reset the type, and bring it home for her grandmother to touch— this time successfully.

No heedless, arrogant scoundrel would ever ruin her again.

Chapter Two

"The trouble, Anthony, is that you have not found the perfect woman," said Charles Camlann Westfall, the Earl of Bedwyr.

Captain Anthony Masinter, late of the Royal Navy, cast a glance at Lady Bedwyr across the parlor.

"Can't agree with you, friend," he said gallantly. "Seems to me she's in this very room."

Lord Bedwyr turned his attention to his lady, whose head was bent to letter writing.

"The perfect woman for *you*." Cam's gaze lingered upon his wife and his entire bearing seemed to change, to grow at once taut as though he were readying for battle and as languid as the lace cuffs spilling from the wrists of his coat.

Four years of marriage and still besotted, poor chap.

Tony didn't go in for that *perfect woman* nonsense. In addition to the rules of the Royal Navy, he lived by one self-imposed rule: treat every woman with utter courtesy and never get within leagues of an altar. That hadn't been difficult to accomplish while at sea. But in the six months since his dear departed great-aunt gave Maitland Manor to him, he had been home, where hopeful maidens abounded. He liked a pretty girl as much as the next man, but he steered clear of matchmaking mamas and their lovely young leg shackles.

His already sick stomach twisted into a bowline knot.

Blast it.

Perfect or not, there was only one woman for him now. He knew what he had to do, even if the mere thought of it made him want to head for open sea.

By golly, there was an idea! He would rejoin and ask to be posted to the East Indies. The admirals said if he ever returned they'd give him any mission he liked. Then he would leave her and the little ones at Maitland Manor, with as much money and as many servants as they needed to live like a merry band, perfectly happy without him.

"The captain does not wish to marry, my lord," Lady Bedwyr said. "He prefers bachelorhood."

She was not *wrong*.

"I preferred bachelorhood as well," Cam replied. "Once upon a time."

Tony frowned into his glass of brandy.

He couldn't rejoin, of course. Not without his first lieutenant, John Park, who at this moment was being readied for burial in dirt. *Travesty.* No naval officer who had served England *and his captain* so faithfully should be put to rest in the earth.

Two tiny hurricanes whirled into the parlor.

"Mama, Letty says I may not braid her doll's hair!"

"Margaret always tangles it up!" her sister hollered.

One golden blond, the other ivory and ebony, the twins looked up at the countess with identically pleading eyes.

"Girls," Lady Bedwyr said calmly, "we have a caller."

"Uncle Anthony!"

"Captain!"

They launched themselves at him. Into his lap they leapt, one wrapping her little arms about his neck and the other presenting him with the abused doll.

"See what Margaret's done, Captain!" Letty exclaimed. "She's ruined Bella's hair."

"Well, I don't know about that," he said, examining the matted mess of silk. "Daresay there's a comb about the house somewhere."

"But combing will tear it all out," Letty said.

"Then she shall wear a wig like Lady Rowden," Margaret stated.

Letty's little brow got dark.

"Here's what," Tony said. "I happen to be acquainted with a pair of dolls searching for two little girls of their own. What say you ladies if I bring them over and introduce all of you?"

"Hurrah!" Margaret exclaimed, tightening her arms about his neck.

"Thank you, Captain," Letty said fervently. "We shall be most, most happy to meet them."

Tony's throat was too tight, and not only from Margaret's snug little arms. He could not be fonder of these mites. But he wasn't ready for three of his own. Not all at once. Not *all of the sudden.*

Even more importantly, he didn't want a wife. He'd always been as happy as a drunken sailor on his own, even when he wasn't actually drunk. Now that his friends were all knotted up in wedded bliss, he was delighted to enjoy the fruits of their domestic tranquility while avoiding it entirely himself.

But he could not avoid *this.*

This was not for pleasure. This was for honor.

From across the parlor he felt his friend's studying gaze. Blast it, but he shouldn't have come here. Not today. Not in this muddle.

The earl rose to his feet. "Come, poppets. Let us find your sister and invite her for a stroll in the park."

They clambered down from Tony's knees.

"Care to join us, Anthony?" the earl said as the little girls took their father's hands.

Tony shook his head. "I'll beg off this time."

The trio went from the parlor.

"Will you dine with us *en famille* tonight?" The countess's soft foreign vowels rolled over the words.

"Afraid I can't." Tony set down the glass of brandy untasted. The stuff would never taste the same again. How many times rolling on the deep, without another sail in sight, had he urged his first officer to relax and enjoy a peaceful moment of well-deserved leisure? But John Park had been dedicated to his work and devoted to his captain. It hadn't been until Tony insisted that his lieutenant finally gave a try to enjoying himself like a regular fellow.

Once introduced to the card table, though, John had not

enjoyed himself. He had lost himself.

Two years later, it killed him.

"Previous engagement." *A funeral*. He climbed to his feet. "Much obliged, though."

"Anthony," she said. "What troubles you?"

His own idiocy.

"Naught that I can't fix, my lady." He bowed. His stomach ached. His head ached. His chest ached. By God, this was almost worse than war.

He took his leave of the countess, barely seeing the familiar street as he mounted his horse, or the people he passed who greeted him. Across his vision instead were Mrs. Park's horrified eyes the night before as he'd told her to hurry, her threadbare gown, the shabby flat, and the three urchins crying for her attention, all of them bone-thin because their father had spent his every penny—*and more*—on the tables.

If John had come to him earlier, he could have helped. He could have done something. If he'd only known before yesterday...

But he had not. He hadn't even seen John Park since January, when they brought the *Victory* into port.

Now he would do the honorable thing. Now he would make it right.

After the funeral.

Tomorrow.

Tomorrow he would ask his former first officer's widow to marry him.

~o0o~

The orbs of Elle's eyes would not function properly. Her gaze stuck as though by glue to the drainage grate cemented into the cobbles of the alley before her toes.

Fifty-three.

The number of pieces of type irretrievably lost.

Fifty-three.

Not five. Or three. Either of which might be overlooked.

Perhaps. But *fifty-three.*

At both dawn and dusk the day before when the traffic was light, then again this morning, she had searched in every crack between cobbles. In vain. So she had returned to the shop and repaired the frame. Then she had reset the text of Lady Justice's latest broadsheet perfectly, down to the exact mistakes recorded on the proof-corrected page she had read to her grandmother.

Mr. Brittle did not allow her to set type. Of course she knew how to do it. Even before she took the position at Brittle & Sons her grandfather, a pressman in the governor of Virginia's printing shop for thirty years, had taught her everything he knew. At his knee, her bedtime stories had not been about knights or princesses, but quoins, scrapers, ink-balls, tympans, formes, and platens.

At Brittle & Sons, it was Charlie's task to compose the type, and occasionally Jo Junior's. Despite Elle's eight years at the shop, Mr. Brittle Senior did not believe that women were intelligent enough for the task. The press was far too valuable, he said.

Far too valuable.

Thirty-nine individual letters, two common words, four spaces, and five punctuation marks were still missing. And the most distressing part: three pieces of type she had recovered were mangled, crushed beneath the hooves of the scoundrel's horse.

Fifty-three pieces in all.

For fifty-three scraps of metal she would lose her position and be sent to prison. She had no doubt Jo Junior would make it so.

Sitting on her haunches in the deepening shadows, staring at the grate through which the missing pieces had tumbled, as numbness settled in she wondered if Mr. Curtis would take in her grandmother, perhaps into some unused corner of the foundling home attached to the church. He was a kind man. He would not allow Gram to be sent to the poorhouse. Not *now.* Perhaps just until…

She squeezed her eyes shut.

Hooves clopped onto the cobbles at the far end of the alley, echoing between the close walls of the buildings to either side. They grew louder as they neared, moving slowly. As the rider passed by a yard away, Elle glanced up. She recognized the horse. And her numb body lit like dry kindling.

The tight springs of her knees uncoiled.

"Why couldn't you have *walked* by two nights ago?" It was more accusation than query.

The hoof clacks halted, the animal's tail swished back and forth once, and the rider swiveled his head and looked directly at her.

Handsomer than she remembered.

Of course he was. Handsome men were the most heedless of others.

Then she saw the uniform: blue and white, medals pinned across his chest, a gold epaulette on one shoulder, a plumed hat, right down to a bejeweled sword on his hip.

"You are a *sailor?*" She did not know where the words came from. She had never spoken to a man in this manner. Not even Jo Junior. "I might have known."

For a moment he stared blankly at her with those violently blue eyes. Then the light in them changed, as though he were bringing her into focus.

"Beg pardon, miss?" His voice was entirely unlike two nights earlier, not booming or commanding, but deep and pleasing in a warm-basket-of-freshly-baked-muffins sort of way. So pleasing that she blinked in surprise.

That surprise overcame her for a only moment.

"Now you beg my pardon? *Now?* When two nights ago, if you had had any consideration for anybody other than yourself, I would not even be here to see you stroll leisurely down this alley *now.*"

"Miss, are you perfectly—" Abruptly he tilted his head forward and his very finely shaped lips parted. "Good God," he uttered. "I nearly ran you over two nights ago. Right here. Entirely forgot till this moment." A furrow creased his handsome brow. "Have you been standing here since then?" The woman's eyes, full of blazing disdain, went round as capstans—soft little brown capstans surmounted by twinkling candles.

"You—You—You," she stuttered, her pretty pink lips pursing in an O upon each syllable. "You, sir, are a *scoundrel.*"

Tony had no doubt of that.

"Now, it was an honest mistake," he said nevertheless. "You're clearly whole and hale and—"

"A *mistake?* You sink a person into ruin and call it a mistake?"

"Royal Navy, miss. With all due respect, sinking people is what I do best." Tony dismounted. He wasn't in any humor for a harangue. But by damn, with color staining her cheeks and her eyes lit with feeling, this girl was the prettiest thing he'd seen in weeks. Months. He needed to examine her more closely. And he was entirely guilty as accused. "I'd no notion you were there and I happened to be in something of a hurry." He took a step toward the girl.

She jerked backward. "Oh? To where were you riding in reckless haste? Your *club?*" She spat the word with such disgust he practically felt it upon his skin.

"Point of fact, no. I was— Well, it don't matter."

"It *does not* matter."

"Glad we agree."

"*Of course* it matters, you illiterate."

Her eyes sparked like fire. It had such an abrupt effect on his cock he almost didn't care that she'd used his family's favorite epithet for him. Almost.

"Now there, miss, what matters is that I'm dashed sorry I startled you."

"Startled does not begin to describe what I—" Her voice broke and this time he was certain he felt it, but not upon his skin, rather beneath his ribs. "Ohh," rushed from between those pretty lips. "Go away. Go away and leave me alone to my fate." All the fight seemed to drain out of her. Lifting a limp hand, she covered her eyes and heaved in an enormous breath. It was an uncomfortable series of movements, obviously alien to her lithe limbs.

With a heavy tread, she started off.

"Miss, if you'll allow me to—"

"I am walking away now. If you follow me, I will call the Watch."

"No Watch on this block at this time of night."

She pivoted around. "Is that a threat? What do you intend to do, sir? Since you have already flattened me against a wall and ruined my life, do you now intend to accost me as well?"

"No."

Abruptly he looked so stern and harsh, Elle did not wonder that he was a decorated officer. With that hard jaw and those intense eyes he might intimidate any sailor into submission.

"You're clearly distraught," he said.

"You noticed that, did you?"

"I'd like to make certain you're all right." He bowed gorgeously. The sword on his hip glittered.

She stared.

But Jo Junior had said all sorts of pretty things, too, before he had used and discarded her and then tried to blackmail her. And she knew better than to trust a sailor.

"I am fine," she said firmly, turned, and walked around the corner. He did not follow her. Of course he did not. A man like that, with aristocrat stamped all over his face, would never actually care about the misery of a common shopgirl.

Beneath the marquee of Brittle & Sons, she unlocked the door, stepped inside, and released a long, shuddering breath.

In the back room, she lit a lamp and carried it to the press. Tracing the beloved backward letters and words with her gaze, she set her fingers to the edge of the frame. Then she closed her eyes and let her fingertips run along the lines of type. It was unwise. She would have to clean the type thoroughly now or the oils from her skin would poorly affect the ink. But she had to feel what her grandmother would have felt if she had been successful two nights earlier, to *feel* Lady Justice and Peregrine's passion in her flesh.

The surface of the composed type was at once pleasurable against her skin and sharp. Just as their public flirtation was. Their romance. So often she and Gram spoke of the day when the anonymous authors would finally reveal their true identities to each other. Someday.

But with each day Gram grew weaker. And yesterday she had spoken of seeing Grandfather again soon. *Seeing* him.

Thickness clogged Elle's throat.

The door of the shop opened. Snatching her fingers back from the type, she went into the front room. The sailor filled the doorway, his hat beneath his arm and a glass of frothy ale in his grip.

"What are you—"

In firm strides he came toward her, grasped her hand, and pressed the glass into it.

"Drink this."

He smelled positively delicious, like rich red wine mingled with fresh cedar. His hand encompassing hers was large, strong, and warm.

"Drink," he repeated in his commanding tone, and released her.

"You brought ale? For me?" She stared into the glass and then up at him. The air went straight out of her lungs. She had never stood so close to a man like this—except once, and she had tried to block that out of her memory.

This man was so . . . *masculine*, from his taut jaw to the slightly curling locks of ebony hair dipping over his brow. His skin was tanned and the tiny lines radiating from the corners of his eyes gave him an air of gravity and perpetual pleasure at once.

"From the King's Barrel?" she managed to say.

"Got to put some color back in those pretty cheeks." His eyes were so blue, vividly blue, like the perfect azure she had seen in pictures of the Mediterranean Sea.

She stepped back, thrusting out the ale toward him. "I do not drink spirits."

"Ale ain't spirits. And you'll drink this."

"Sir, you might well be in the navy, but I am not and I needn't follow your—"

"*Drink.* Then you'll tell me what troubles you and I'll make it right."

Sheer shock from this declaration sent the glass toward her mouth and the first sip of ale down her throat.

She coughed. "This is *not* ale."

"Little something extra in there. Calms the nerves. Drink." Setting his hat upon Jo Junior's desk, then crossing his arms over his decorated chest, he sat back against the edge of the furniture and watched her venture another sip, then another. She felt assessed, like he might take the measure of an unexpected ship that appeared on the horizon. As she swallowed a fifth and then a sixth sip of ale—and something extra—warmth gathered in her belly and spread softly to her head. His lips shifted upward at one corner.

He had very fine lips. *Very* fine. Beautiful.

She blinked.

This was the reason she never drank ale.

"Now," he said, "tell me." His voice was like the rumble of a very large cat, almost a purr, a lion's purr.

Ale was the devil's brew.

She shoved the glass forward. He shook his head. She moved around him and set it down on Jo Junior's desk with a decisive clack. The sailor turned to watch her.

"I'm waiting," he purred.

"I suppose you will not leave until I have told you."

"You suppose right."

"*Correctly.* I suppose correctly."

He grinned. His teeth were beautifully white and straight, his smile positively brilliant. Perhaps it was his tan skin, or the crisp blue of his coat and snowy white of his neckcloth and waistcoat, or his arms crossed nonchalantly across his chest so that she could see the pull of fabric against muscle . . . Despite the ale, her throat went dry.

She backed away a step. "You have ruined me."

The blue eyes flicked down her body, then up again before his grin broadened.

"Fairly certain I'd recall that," he said.

Her cheeks flamed. "That was not, of course, what I meant by those words."

His eyes laughed. "You don't say?"

"You *are* a scoundrel, sir."

"Assuredly. Now tell me your trouble and I'll do my scoundrelly best to solve it."

"You will do your *scoundrel's* best."

"Aye." He uncrossed his arms and set his hands to either side of him on the edge of the desk. They were strong, big hands, and the sight of them made Elle's insides even warmer than the ale that was clouding her head.

Pivoting away, she went through the connecting door into the press room. His boot steps followed, even and easy.

Halting before the press, she said, "This. This is my trouble. You—you *and I*—caused it."

When after a moment he said nothing, she looked up at his face. He was studying the huge machine made of wood and metal like he had studied her, but with a guarded frown.

"Not quite clear on the trouble, miss."

"That, sir, is the trouble." She pointed to a slender blank space inside the chase. "And that." Her fingertip located another empty spot. "And that. And the fifty other missing pieces of type."

"Pieces of *type*?" He pronounced the word as though it were foreign.

"The metal bits used in printing. This is a printing house. Or hadn't you noticed?"

"I did. Just don't know much about it," he said with diffidence that did not suit him. Then his lips curved into the dashing grin again. "Teach me, why don't you?"

Plucking out a sliver of type, she brandished it. "This is type. Each piece is a letter or symbol or blank space, or a common word."

"Common word?"

"The. And. At. In."

"Aha."

"Together, arranged properly, they comprise the words and sentences of any printed matter. Each folio of a book, for instance, must be composed and printed individually. Then they are all bound together. It is the same with a newspaper or journal."

He nodded, glancing from her fingertips holding the piece to the chase. "Fancy that."

She loved everything about printing, the precision of it, the beauty of a carefully composed page, the scent of ink, and the comfort of this room when a work was in progress and pages were draped all about, the ink drying. It had been an eon, however, since she had seen it the way he was clearly seeing it now: as a novelty.

"What's this book?" He gestured to the forme.

"It is not a book page. It is Lady Justice's next publication." She did not bother hiding the pride in her voice. Everybody in London knew Brittle & Sons published the pamphleteer. Lady Justice was so popular, and her identity such a carefully guarded secret, Mr. Brittle and his sons had turned away dozens of bribery offers for information about her. The Brittles did not even know her true identity; everything she wrote came to the shop via anonymous couriers. Even the letters that Peregrine sent to Lady Justice traveled such a circuitous route that nobody had succeeded at tracing it.

"Hm," the sailor said without any sign of awe.

"Lady Justice," she repeated. "Britain's premier pamphleteer."

His face was blank.

"You have heard of her, haven't you?" she said.

"Daresay everybody has." He folded his arms again across his chest.

"But . . ." London was mad about Lady Justice, either with adoration or outrage. Elle had never encountered anybody who did not have a strong opinion about her one way or the other. "You have read her pamphlets, haven't you?"

"Can't say that I have," he said. "This—" He waved his hand over the press. "This is hers?"

"Yes, although that section"—she pointed—"is Peregrine's latest letter. She included it within her piece, as she often does when aristocrats write to her."

"Peregrine. That fellow she's always quarreling with?"

"Yes. Although I would not exactly call it quarreling."

"What would you call it?"

"You *have* read her pamphlets. You are only pretending to be unimpressed so that you can keep the upper hand here, aren't you?"

His gaze came to her, clear and direct. "Don't know about any upper hand, but no, I haven't read 'em. Heard plenty about 'em, though. Fellow can't drink a bottle at his club these days without having to listen to some old lord raging about *Madame la* Justice's radical notions and some young cub defending her till he's blue in the face."

Elle smiled at this evidence of her hero's notoriety.

"Many good men admire her." That her work helped Lady Justice's voice reach thousands of Britons with every broadsheet Brittle & Sons printed filled her with satisfaction.

"But you like him," he said. "Don't you?"

"Him?"

He motioned again to the press, his brows canting up. "The hawk man."

"Peregrine?" she said. "No. I—"

"Heard it in your voice when you said his name. His pen name, that is."

"What?" Warmth was flooding into her cheeks. "No. I— What did you hear?"

"Softness," he said. "You admire him."

"I admire *her*. The reforms she propounds are meant for the good of all Britons. He disagrees with her about everything, of course."

"You like him."

"I don't."

His lips curved into the gentlest smile. "If you say so." He nodded toward the machine. "Now, what's upset you about this type?"

For a moment as he studied the forme she stared at him, and understood how he must command men aboard ship: not with intimidation or even with severity, but with a natural, subtle shift from thoroughly focusing on a person's face and feelings to the business at hand. If she were not so peculiarly sensitized by the ale she would not have noticed it.

"The other night," she said, "I was carrying this chase— this frame full of type—down the street. When you galloped by, I was so startled that I dropped it, and it broke. Yesterday I collected the pieces of type, but I have not been able to retrieve them all."

"How many pieces are missing?"

"Fifty-three." Abruptly her stomach felt like lead again.

"This don't seem like a particularly long page."

"This *does not* seem like a particularly *lengthy* page," she mumbled. "It is not, in fact."

"Must be more type somewhere." He looked past the press. "There." As though he could see through the back of the huge case on the other side of the machine, he went around to the front of it and drew off the cover, revealing a sloped tray of dozens of little open boxes of type.

"Here's a veritable mess of the stuff," he said. "Why don't you fill in the holes and that'll be that?"

Her chest felt like lead too now. She went to his side and stared down at the tray. Most of the boxes were still nearly full of type.

"I could. But my employers will discover the missing type when they return from holiday in a fortnight."

"Wondered about that detail," he murmured. "Don't seem the sort of girl to steal right out from under somebody's nose."

"What is that supposed to mean? That I am cunning?"

His attention shifted from the type to her face. "No. That you're intelligent."

"Oh." She could not hold his gaze. "This publication is quite brief. When we set the pages of large books, though, this tray is often nearly empty. But it is more than that. My crime is twofold. I should never have taken the chase out of the shop to begin with. Not even out of this room. Even if I had not lost any pieces of type, if my employers discover that I borrowed them for a few hours they would have grounds for terminating me."

"Well, then why not purchase the type that's gone missing? They needn't ever know of this little mishap."

"I wish I could! The type for this particular press cannot be replaced easily." Even if she could afford such a purchase. The happy haze from the ale had entirely dissipated. "There are few such presses in all of Britain. It is an original Warburg, and only three were sent to England from Germany. It is an extraordinarily valuable machine, Mr. . . ." She looked up, past his broad, blue-clad shoulder decorated with a gold epaulette, to his handsome face, and her tongue went dry. "Lieutenant . . ."

"Captain," he said in his marvelously deep and easy voice, the full, glorious force of his intensely beautiful gaze not upon her eyes. But on her lips. "Captain Anthony Masinter, miss. At your service."

One of her feet fell back. Then the other. "You should not be here. You should go." She dragged her gaze away and went to the door. "You must go. Now. Please."

"Can't." He remained where he stood. "Not without first finding a solution to this."

"No. There is no solution. None. I shall simply have to suffer the consequences of my crime."

"Daresay crime's giving it a bit too much drama. Determined, though, to help you work this out." He moved toward her, all six-and-more-feet of gorgeous, well-muscled masculinity. A spike of sharp, hot panic jolted up her middle.

She darted into the front room, snatched his hat off the desk, and shoved it into his chest. "You cannot help. You obviously know nothing about printing."

"No, but—"

"Even if you did, there is nothing to be done anyway." She thrust wide the shop door. Without, the night had fallen sultry and dark, the usual sounds of the King's Barrel spilling onto the street. "Please, Captain," she said through gritted teeth. "Go."

"But I—"

"You have really done enough already," she said sharply. "Haven't you?"

For a moment he seemed to consider her again. Then he bent his head, set his hat atop his glossy black locks, and went out.

Elle closed the door, bolted it, and fell against the edge of the desk where a captain in the Royal Navy had sat minutes earlier.

"Never again," she whispered fervently, her gaze slipping through the doorway to the far corner of the press room, where once she had allowed foolish weakness toward a handsome man to overcome her good sense. Straightening up, she brushed her skirts free of the taint of *that* man's desk and stepped away from it. Because of that weakness, because of what happened afterward, Josiah Brittle Junior, had it in for her.

His smiling lies and seductive grins had coaxed her into trusting him. Then came the heartbreak when he returned from a trip to Edinburgh married. Then—when she refused to give him again what she had while in the throes of naïve adoration—began his vendetta against her, a vendetta that he still held onto tightly, five years later. She could already see his triumphant grin, when the family returned and he discovered the missing type, and hear him condemning her to his father and brother, and then throwing her out onto the street.

She would never again fall for a pretty face.

Captain Anthony Masinter was not pretty. He was worse. He was the sort of man Lady Justice despised: attractive, privileged, elite, obviously wealthy, and entirely at ease with his mastery over everybody. She needed his help like she needed a fresh new hole in her heart.

Her heart was already sufficiently full of holes.

"Never again," she said loudly to the empty shop—no matter how tempting the man and his offer to help. "Never, ever again."

Chapter Three

She was the prettiest thing he had ever seen, in a heap of trouble he'd caused, and more disdainful than the Duchess of Hammershire on her tetchiest days.

He had to help her. Even if she didn't want help.

There were three things Tony knew without doubt: how to command a man-of-war to victory in battle, how to turn a glum body to lighter spirits, and how to solve tricky problems. For this sassy-tongued printing-shop mistress with troubled eyes he'd haul out the twelve-pounders if it meant she'd direct that smile at him again.

Leaving behind Gracechurch Street and the girl whose name he didn't even know yet, he turned away from the part of town where his first lieutenant had once lived and toward his own house instead. He couldn't very well go beg the widow's hand with his head full of another woman. And Mrs. Park probably needed a day or two to come to terms with the state in which her husband had left her and their children: broke.

He would find a solution to the pretty print mistress's bind, and then—afterward—see about the other woman's horrid situation that was also his fault.

But by the time his manservant, Cob, set the post beside his coffee and steak the following morning, he still had not devised a solution. Taking up a letter marked with his name in a familiar flowing hand, he passed it back to Cob.

"Do the honors, old fellow?"

His manservant opened the message and read aloud.

Darling,

Cob cleared his throat, then continued.

Uncle Frederick is crawling out of his hole to attend Lady Beaufetheringstone's ball tomorrow evening. No other hostess can ever summon him forth; I think he must have a tendre for her. But I know he will be delighted to see you.

Tony snorted above the rim of his coffee cup. "Delighted" went too far. His mother's brother, Bishop Frederick Baldwin, was as much of a snob as the rest of the family. But Tony could always make the old prelate laugh, or better yet, turn red and holler.

I expect to meet you there. Save a dance for me.
Bisous,
Seraphina
P.S. Do wear your uniform. You know how I adore it when the ladies flock about you like gulls around a topsail.

Tony smiled. Seraphina was the only member of his family who acknowledged his chosen profession. The others preferred to pretend that he'd been on an extended educational trip abroad. For twenty years.

He would attend the ball. Uncle Frederick was a cranky old codger, but Tony enjoyed him. He enjoyed everybody, mostly.

He wanted to enjoy a snappy-tongued, doe-eyed print mistress, however, more than he had ever before wanted to enjoy a respectable woman.

Her sweet, lush pink lips had entranced him. And her slender fingers, so graceful yet purposeful on that machine . . . He'd gotten downright lightheaded watching her hands move. And hard. Right there in that shop he had imagined removing the pins from her tightly bound hair the color of Russian sable, sinking his hands into it, and tilting her face up to his.

"*Captain,*" his manservant said.

"Cob?"

"I said, would you care for me to reply to Lady Beaufetheringstone's invitation to the ball, which has been waiting for your consideration, unopened on the foyer table, for a fortnight—"

"If it's unopened, how do you know it's an invitation to a ball?"

"—or to Mrs. Starling's letter?"

"No need. Lady B don't stand on ceremony, and Seri knows that if she asks I'll attend."

"Very well, sir. And when do you wish to meet with the land steward from Maitland Manor?"

"Right." He was now the owner of his dearly departed great-aunt's house, including its lucrative lands. With a tidy bundle in his bank that he had accumulated at sea, he was set for life on land like a veritable nabob . . . while John Park was underground. "Have him come tomorrow."

"Very good, Captain." Cob gave a smart bow and retired from the breakfast chamber.

Maitland Manor was a dashed fine estate. Now he was going to set up a family in that house. A ready-made family.

He toyed with the corner of Seraphina's note. Then, like lost treasure washing up on shore, a solution to the pretty print mistress's conundrum occurred to him.

Bolting from his chair, he grabbed his hat and headed for the mews.

~o0o~

When the door of the shop burst open, Elle had just folded her umbrella and bent to remove her boots. The summer sky was pouring down rain in slanting sheets, and she had returned from her regular weekly tea with Minnie, Adela, and Esme soaked through. In a whirl of rain and wind, Captain Masinter swept in, knocking her off balance. She flailed, he grabbed her arms, and abruptly she was looking up at very close range into a face that was even handsomer in the light of the gray day than by lamp-lit night.

"Good day, ma'am." His smile glittered and his eyes were so full of pleasure that she could not make her tongue function. She wrenched out of his hold and backed away. She had barely managed to cease thinking of him since the night before. This was not a pleasant surprise.

"Why are you here?" she demanded.

His smile did not falter. Sweeping off his hat, he moved toward her.

"I've devised a solution." His gaze traversed her from hair to hem, lingering on her stockinged feet soaking up rain on the floor. "Why aren't you wearing shoes?"

"I have just come in from— My business is none of yours, sir." She searched around the floor for her slippers.

Grabbing them up, he went to one knee on the damp boards and proffered a shoe.

"Hand on my shoulder," he said.

Her mouth hung open.

"Come now." He wiggled the slipper. "Can't tell you my capital idea with you standing there shoeless."

"Captain Masinter, this is—"

"Serendipitous!"

"Serendipitous?"

"I'll explain it all as soon as you're shod."

There was nothing to do but set her palm gingerly on his gloriously hard shoulder, slip her feet into the proffered slippers, and try to ignore the delicious tingle that leaped from his fingertips brushing across her insole right up into her belly. Shod and breathless, she backed away as he stood to his full height again.

"You have ruined your—that is—your—" She simply could not say the word breeches. Not to a man she did not know. She pointed to his knees.

"Sailor, miss. A bit of damp's nothing." He waved it away. "Good God, woman, aren't you eager to hear my plan? Moment I came up with it I could barely contain myself. Wished I'd had wings to fly here."

"Impetuosity does not seem like a very useful trait for a

ship captain," she mumbled.

"*Au contraire*, madam. All great sea commanders have got to be able to throw themselves into a fine idea at a moment's notice. That's how battles are won."

"Are you a great sea commander, Captain Masinter?" She already knew. Casually introducing the Royal Navy into conversation at tea with her friends, she had learned from Adela, who was silly with adoration for all men in uniform, and Minnie, who practically memorized the gossip columns, that Captain Anthony Masinter, recently retired from his command of the *Victory*, was a bona fide war hero. Apparently, he had also lately come into an impressive fortune. None of this had been welcome news to Elle. She did not need more reasons to dream about the stranger who had ruined her life. And she adamantly did not trust sailors.

But now she was not dreaming of this sailor. She was staring up at him like a nincompoop.

"Came out of a few routs intact," he replied easily. "But that's not important at present, of course. Now see here, miss—" Abruptly he sobered. "Know it ain't proper—"

"It *is not* proper."

"—to ask you to give me the honor of your name, but this'd all be much easier if I knew it."

"What would be easier?"

"Helping you out of this bind."

"No." She backed away. "I told you last night that I do not need your help."

He watched as she retreated another step.

"You know," he said, "you needn't always be running away from me. I won't bite. And I'm dashed sorry to disagree with you, but it seems you do need help."

But she did not believe that he would not bite. Men always bit when they discovered a woman unprotected and alone. From the moment her father had sold her mother's leather tooled Holy Bible to buy gin, to the day Jo Junior reappeared in London with a wife, all Elle had ever known of men were lies. Except her grandfather, but he had been a man of letters.

"Why are you doing this?" she demanded. "What do you hope to gain from it?"

"What—Why—" he began twice, then more slowly, seriously: "Your continued future employment in this shop, of course. That is what you want, isn't it?"

"That is all? You do not want anything else?"

For a moment the ship captain was silent. Then he said, "No. I want nothing else." With a tilt of his head forward and a very slight upturning of the corner of his lips, he added, "Miss . . . ?"

She did not believe him. But he believed himself, and that was better than nothing. Also, he was correct: she did need help.

"Miss Flood," she said.

He smiled with such clear contentment that she wished she believed him too.

"Great pleasure to make your acquaintance, Miss Flood." He bowed. Today he had left off his uniform and wore instead a coat that fit his broad shoulders to perfection, dark breeches, and well-used although perfectly polished boots. If not for his tan she would have assumed him merely an aristocrat, a man perhaps more comfortable in the country than town, but wealthy and elite nonetheless. She must be mad to have imagined he wanted anything from her—anything of the sort that Jo Junior wanted. A man like this did not need to go trawling among the common class; he could have any woman among the glittering beau monde that he liked. She need not have worried.

Then his gaze dipped to her lips and destroyed her certainty about that.

"No," she said flatly. "This is a mistake. I can see to this myself." She went to the door, opened it to the rain, and gestured him out. "Please go, Captain."

"Charming enactment of déjà vu, ma'am. But I'd rather drown in the indoor flood than the outdoor one."

"Captain, please."

"Miss Flood—"

"*No.* No and no. I have thought it all out, you see. Every possible solution. And unless you plan on petitioning the city to drill through the concrete to wrest that drainage grate from the street, you can offer no solution that will serve. Anyway, today's rain has blocked even that far-fetched avenue of hope, for if any pieces had fallen into that drain, with this deluge they have surely been washed further down the pipes, perhaps even to the Thames already. So you see, Captain, there is no need for you to—"

He was upon her so swiftly she hadn't even time to protest. Grabbing the door with one hand he swung it shut. Then both of her hands were in his, entirely encompassed in warm strength, and, despite the shock of it, *not at all uncomfortable.*

"Miss Flood," he said very soberly, "resolve yourself to my assistance in this matter. And then, if you could see your way to sharing with me your given name, I would account myself the most fortunate of men. That, and it'd make this whole thing a lot less formal." He smiled. "What say you?"

She was a fool to allow it. But she would be a bigger fool to reject help.

"You will not go away, even if I demand it?" she tried a final time.

"Given who's at fault here, I truly would be a scoundrel to desert you now."

"My name is Gabrielle."

"Gabrielle." Upon his tongue it sounded like a caress, deep and seductive. "Lovely name, like the lady who bears it." Abruptly he released her and backed away, disposing himself once again quite comfortably on the surface of Jo Junior's desk. "Now, as to my idea, me and you will—"

"You and I."

"Precisely. Me and you—"

"*You* and *I.* Not me and you."

"What in the devil? It's the same two people."

"I am not a 'two people' with you, Captain." Moving around his outrageously muscular outstretched legs, she removed him from her sightline. It was considerably easier to talk to him when she could not see him. "Despite my reluctant agreement to accept your help, we are not a 'we,'" she insisted. "You are a scoundrel—"

He chuckled.

"—and I must devise a method of crawling into that sewage drain in order to—"

"That's what I've been trying to say." He followed her into the press room. "I've got an idea to replace those bits and it don't require crawling about in drainpipes to accomplish it."

"It *does not* require crawling about in drainpipes. Your blithe use of improper grammar is an abomination of the English language and good manners." Her head snapped around. "It doesn't?"

He peered at her carefully, his gaze traveling over her from the crown of her bedraggled bonnet to the sodden hem of her skirt.

"A man's allowed to misuse grammar every so often, ain't—*isn't* he?"

"Not unless he wishes to sound like a cretin. Why are you looking at me like that?"

"Fact is," he said thoughtfully, "this little project's going to require the opposite of crawling through drainpipes."

"The opposite?" She frowned, making a delicate crease in a brow that had suffered far too many creases lately, Tony thought, or perhaps—given the sorry old state of her accoutrements—always.

Not this time.

"Last night," he said, "when you mentioned the name of this machine's maker, War—"

"Warburg?"

"Right, Warburg. I thought it sounded familiar."

"Unless you are an aficionado of printing technology—which we have previously established you are not—I fail to see how that name could be familiar to you, Captain."

"Not an aficionado myself, no. But I've got an uncle who's a collector."

"A collector of printing presses?" she said, her pretty eyes decidedly skeptical as she untied her bonnet and revealed the coils of midnight satin he'd spent hours fantasizing about since the night before. Unbound. Flowing over his hands. Spread out on a pillow.

"A collector of all sort of knickknacks and whatnot, actually," he said, ignoring the tightness gathering in his breeches. "So happens that when my cousin and I were little mites we'd spend hours 'n' hours lost in that collection. Uncle Frederick hates any of it to leave the house. But he never minded it when Seri and I rummaged about, as long as we left everything as we found it."

"And?"

"And dashed if I don't recall a box in that collection that was precisely like this one"—he gestured to the printing press—"full of type."

"A box full of type? Do you mean to say a chase with set type? Really?" Her eyes had gone round again, and sparkly. When she looked him like that, he felt like he was on the quarterdeck, every sail full, in a following wind. He nodded.

"But there are many makers of printing presses," she said. "Type that has been cast for one press will not necessarily fit into another."

"Suspected that. This one had a name carved into the side of it. W-A-R," he said slowly, so as not to bungle it, "B-U-R-G." He crossed his arms. "Daresay it's still right where it used to be. Uncle Frederick never moves a thing, just piles up new on top of the old."

Instead of throwing herself into his arms and declaring her undying gratitude, she reached for a pair of pliers and came at his groin.

"Now, miss," He backed up a step. "No need to—"

She plied them to the side of the machine in front of him. With a few quick twists of her wrist, the outside edge of the frame loosened. Her slender, strong fingers tugged away a brace alongside the frame and he was almost too distracted imagining those fingers on him to see what she'd revealed.

WARBURG. Emblazoned along the side of the box of type. She turned her face up to him and her eyes looked odd— almost watery but not quite.

"Now, don't go weeping," he said with a smile. "We ain't accomplished the thing yet."

"We *have not* accomplished it yet," she said with a little grin. "And I never weep, Captain."

"Ever?" He wanted to reach up and stroke a loose tendril of hair from her cheek and feel that smooth skin.

"Never." She dropped her gaze and fiddled with the pliers. "Will you go to your uncle's house and retrieve the type today?" she said, then set down the tool and crossed to the desk to take up a pen. "I will write a list of the letters and symbols that are missing." She dipped the pen into an inkpot. "Then you can take from your uncle's collection only the letters that—"

"No," he said. "That won't do. Best if you pick out the bits you need yourself."

"But—"

"I can't be counted on to get it right."

"Captain, I find it hard to believe that a victorious naval commander could not accomplish such a small task without assistance."

She wouldn't be the only one.

He went toward her, forcing a jaunty grin. "Trust me on this, Gabrielle. It ain't going to be quite as easy as knocking on Uncle Frederick's door."

"It *is not.* Why not?"

He glanced at her gown that had seen better days. Many better days. And yet in the simple frock that displayed her curves without embellishments of laces and whatnot, she looked as sweet to him as a mango tree after a westbound crossing.

But Bishop Frederick Baldwin would take one look at her and turn up his nose.

"My uncle don't like people he don't know coming into his house."

"*Doesn't* know."

"And he *doesn't* go out much. I've got an idea of where he'll be two nights from now, though, and I can introduce you. Then you won't be a stranger. Have you got a ball gown?"

"A ball gown?"

"You know the sort of thing, a fancy dress for—"

"I know what a ball gown is, Captain. For what, pray tell, do you suppose I would ever require such a garment?"

He lifted his brows. "Attending balls?"

Her lush pink lips went perfectly flat. He wanted to kiss them. He wanted to take those lips beneath his and taste every flavor of her sassy mouth. By God, his pulse was flying at ten knots and he wasn't even touching her.

Touching her in that manner, however, was not in the cards for him.

Cards.

Blast it.

Also, she was looking at him like he was a blockhead.

"I suspect I am as likely to have a ball gown, Captain, as you are. Unless you are hiding an interesting secret beneath that coat."

He bit back a grin. "No ball gown, then?"

"No ball gown." She was obviously fighting her own smile.

"I've got an idea."

Chapter Four

With a quick grin and a "Trust me," the captain disappeared into the rain.

He did not reappear that day. Elle had no confidence that he would ever reappear, and no conviction that she wanted him to. And she most certainly did not trust him, no matter that the king and Admiralty obviously did. Only one man had ever deserved her trust, and he was now in heaven.

The following day she invited her friends to the shop to read Lady Justice's latest installment.

"A sweet tongue and a soft caress," Mineola read aloud for the fourth or fifth time, a quiver of excitement in her voice.

"That rules you out, Elle," Adela said with a wry smile.

"That isn't fair, Adela," Esme said, stroking her fingertips along the edge of Charlie's desk. "Elle offered both a sweet tongue and soft caresses to Mr. Josiah Brittle Junior."

"Until he married that rich Scottish papermaker's daughter."

"And broke Elle's heart."

"And left her determined never to fall in love again, which is the most foolish part of it all." Minnie's lower lip poked out. "Really, Elle, you must relent someday."

"If Peregrine appeared at the door of this shop at this very moment," Esme said, "I suspect Elle would leap headfirst into love."

Elle pursed her lips. "You three are a pack of romantic ninnies. If Peregrine did ever appear in this shop—"

The shop door opened and four pairs of eyes went to it, three hoping the caller would be arrogant, aristocratic, and named Peregrine. Elle hoped for a naval hero, despite herself.

Instead the caller was a man of about five decades, rather short, dressed neatly, possessed of a ramrod straight spine, with skin even more deeply tanned than Captain Masinter's.

"Miss Gabrielle Flood?" he said.

Elle stepped forward. "Yes?"

"How do you do? I am Cob." He gestured out the door. "The carriage awaits you."

Her friends' eyes went wide when they saw the vehicle: wheels and panels shining, the pair hitched to it splendid, and the coachman atop the box dressed even more nattily than Mr. Cob.

"The captain wished to escort you," Mr. Cob said. "But he suspected you would prefer not to travel in a closed carriage with a gentleman to whom you are not related."

Minnie gasped. Adela hiccupped. Esme lifted a hand to her mouth.

"Travel to where, Mr. Cob?" Elle's heartbeats were ridiculously quick. She might have anticipated something like this. She should have. Men were, after all, men.

"To Madame Étoile's home." He pronounced the name *Ay-twaal* with perfect French intonation. "She awaits you there to see about a ball gown."

"A ball gown?" Adela breathed.

"Madame Étoile?" Elle said.

"The premier modiste in London," Minnie exclaimed. "Madame Couture complains of her stealing all the most elite customers. Why, Elle, she is famous!"

Elle looked into the astonished eyes of her friend, a seamstress at the modiste's shop three doors down the street, and then at Esme and Adela's astonished faces too.

"I should lock up the shop."

The carriage was as impressive on the inside as on the exterior, with velvet cushions and satiny black tassels. Peering through the glass window, she offered her friends a little wave, and the carriage started off.

When the door opened again it was not Mr. Cob's hand that appeared to assist her but Captain Masinter's.

"How'd you enjoy the ride? Don't have a carriage in town myself. A bachelor don't need one, of course. I supposed you'd prefer a private vehicle to a hackney, and my cousin's rig is bang up to the nines, ain't it?"

"*Isn't* it," she murmured. The street was exceedingly fashionable and entirely residential, with birches heavy with leaves lining the clean-swept avenue. The stoop he gestured her toward was elegant and understated. This was no love nest to which he had conveyed her. This was the home of a gentlewoman of means.

The naval hero, however, was the most attractive part of the scene. Wearing a dark coat and buff trousers, without a hat, he seemed perfectly at ease in the summer sunshine that glimmered in his eyes, and she had no trouble whatsoever imagining him atop the deck of a great ship.

"Your cousin?" was all she could manage.

"You'll meet her inside." He offered his arm.

She placed her fingertips on his elbow and a slight smile creased his cheeks.

"Thank you for sending the carriage," she said.

"There now, that wasn't so hard, was it?"

"What was not?" she said warily.

"Accepting help." His crooked smile showed a wedge of white teeth. "I suspect that you, Miss Gabrielle Flood, are unaccustomed to allowing others to help you."

"I do not trust many people." *Especially men.*

"Trust me," he said so simply, so peacefully, it felt as though she had come in from the cold and he led her to a crackling fire and tucked a cup of tea into her hands.

Then the door was closing behind them and a young woman in flowing robes of every jewel tone imaginable was gliding down the stairs toward them.

"She is just as lovely as you said, Anthony!" she exclaimed in a voice of rich honey. Gliding to Elle, she grasped her hands, spread her arms wide, and her eyes that were as dark as coffee perused Elle from tip to toes. "Oh, yes. Yes," she said. "You will do magnificently."

"Miss Flood," he said, "allow me to present to you my cousin, Madame Étoile. Seraphina, this is the lady whose employment I carelessly put in danger."

"It is a delight to make your acquaintance, Miss Flood," the beauty said. For beautiful the modiste most certainly was, with wide dark eyes, thick hair fixed away from her face with jewel-studded combs and tumbling in soft curls down her back, and skin as tan as the captain's but not, Elle thought, from exposure to sun.

Cousin was far too convenient a term, and he had addressed her familiarly. She was probably his mistress.

The sinking sensation in Elle's stomach made her furious. A fine carriage and a knee-weakening smile were not sufficient grounds upon which to trust a man.

"Magnificently?" she said.

"Magnificently suited for the gown I have been preparing for you since yesterday, of course." She tucked her hand into Elle's arm and guided her toward the stairs. "We shan't need you, Tony," she threw over her shoulder. "Not for hours yet."

"Happy to wait," he said in the same easy tone in which he said everything.

Elle allowed the beauty to lead her up the stairs, casting one swift glance back at the captain. He stood at the base of the staircase, watching her thoughtfully.

In a chamber furnished in pure feminine luxury, with draperies and upholstery of shimmering pink- and cream-colored satin and plush pillows corded in gold, the modiste bade her recline on a divan fit for a queen and tugged on a bellpull. From an adjoining chamber appeared two women garbed elegantly, if not as ostentatiously as Madame Étoile. They proceeded to undress Elle to her shift and spirited her clothing away.

"To be cleaned and pressed while we work," her hostess said, leading her to a tea table laid with the most beautiful porcelain Elle had ever seen—bone white limned in gold with tiny pink flowers—and cakes iced in pastels and gold dust.

"Do take a lemon tart, Miss Flood," one of the assistants

said. "They are scrumptious."

Turning away from the delicacies, Elle said, "I am grateful for your time, Madame Étoile—"

"How charmingly you say my name. Tony did not tell me that you speak French."

"He does not—" She glanced at the waiting assistants and lowered her voice. "He does not know that I speak anything except English. He does not know *me*. But that really is not to the point. Madame Étoile, I am grateful for your time, but the simple fact of it is that I cannot afford your services." She could not afford the iced cakes arranged on the gold and pink plate. She could not afford her grandmother's medicine either. And after the Brittles returned, she would not be able to afford the rent on their flat. Or food. "In truth, I do not even understand why I am here or for what occasion the captain believes I need a ball gown."

"Didn't Tony tell you?" She chuckled and drew Elle forward. "This, Miss Flood, is the gown that you will wear to the ball tomorrow night where you will meet our uncle who so rarely leaves his house that it is a miracle he is attending an event."

Fashioned of silver-shot tulle over an underdress of white silk, and scattered with tiny diamonds and silver sequins like stardust, it had delicate little puff sleeves, a waist that sat tight up to the bodice, and a demi-train trimmed in silver embroidery.

"This cannot be for me."

"Yet it is. Anthony instructed me to dress you to impress. You will have a silver wrap, and white gloves, I think," she added, glancing at Elle's hands. "Silver slippers as well. Penelope will show you reticules later."

"But I cannot afford to pay for this—the gown, wrap, gloves—any of it."

"Oh, you needn't. Anthony feels positively wretched about the accident, and has asked me to do this as a favor to him."

"Someone must pay for it, though. I cannot accept—"

"You cannot accept such a gift from a gentleman, of course. Let us agree, then, that I am passionately eager to see this gown worn by the ideal model, and you are she, so in truth you are doing me a favor." She smiled delightfully. "Now, Miss Flood—may I call you Gabrielle? It suits you so well."

"Did you say 'our uncle'? That is, Captain Masinter's uncle is your uncle as well?"

"Technically, Uncle Frederick is Tony's mother's brother, so I am not truly related to him. But we spent any number of hours in his house when we were children, so I called him Uncle Frederick as well." Her artfully sculpted brows rose.

"My friends call me Elle."

"And you will call me Seraphina." She grasped Elle's hands warmly. "For I have a suspicion we will be good friends. Now, Elle, you must take a lemon tart and a cup of tea. For in no more than ten minutes you will be barred from all food and drink while I fit this gown for you." She looked her up and down again. "Yes. Yes, indeed. What a fine eye for a lady my cousin has."

"A lady?"

"Chocolate, Miss Flood?" Penelope said, placing before Elle a crystal plate adorned with bonbons.

"Why must I look like a lady tomorrow night?" Elle asked Seraphina.

Seraphina smiled mysteriously and drew her to the tea table where Penelope and the other woman urged her to eat while chatting away about silk and satin and stays, and never giving her a moment to ask another question.

~o0o~

Two hours later, Seraphina declared the fitting a success.

"Tomorrow night you will take the *ton* by storm!" She opened the door and drew Elle onto the landing.

"If it serves the purpose, I will be satisfied." In the shimmering gown she had felt like a common duck dressed up in swan's feathers. No one would believe she was an actual lady.

"Finished so soon?" The captain stood at the bottom of the stairs.

"You haven't been in that spot for two hours, have you, Tony?" Seraphina said as they descended.

"Went over to Charles's house to pay a call on the girls," he said, but his gaze was on Elle. "How do you like my cousin's shop?"

The girls? This neighborhood was far too elegant for a brothel.

"Very much." Elle did not understand him, or this world of fashionable society, or the project he had in mind for the following night. But she could not resist the honest pleasure in his eyes.

"Have you heard from Aunt Adelaide lately, Anthony?" Seraphina said.

"Sennight or so ago. Invitation to Father's birthday party. Suppose you've gotten it too."

"I did." Seraphina tilted her head. "Will you drive me?"

"Wasn't planning on going, actually." He glanced away, toward the door. "All sorts of business to take care of here, of course."

"Tony." Seraphina's voice softened. "I cannot miss it. But I will not enjoy it if you are not there."

His eyes turned sharply to her face for a moment. Then he nodded, once, a short conciliatory jerk of his chin. "As you wish."

Seraphina smiled. "Shall I include your reply to the invitation in my own?"

He drew in a tight breath. "Aye." And then: "Thank you."

Seraphina went to him, the diaphanous drapes of her sleeves fluttering, making her progress across the foyer seem like nothing less than the flight of a magnificent bird. She grasped his arm and went onto her tiptoes and kissed him on the cheek. She lingered there.

"You are the bravest man I have ever known, Anthony." It was barely a whisper, but Elle heard it, and a peculiar rush of warmth spread through her body.

Then she saw something she had never seen before, something she had never thought to see: a great big elegantly dressed gentleman scooping up a fine lady in his arms and giving her an enormous bear hug. Seraphina's laughter bubbled over his shoulder.

As he released her and came toward the door, Elle snapped her mouth shut.

"Until tomorrow, Elle," Seraphina said with a conspiratorial grin. "I can hardly wait."

Chapter Five

"Please tell me why I have spent the afternoon being fitted for a ball gown," Elle said when they were some distance away from the modiste's house. He had asked her if she minded his riding in the carriage with her. Now she regretted allowing it. Enclosed in the tight space, even with glass windows on both sides, she felt his nearness too acutely. He was so large and handsome and smelled so deliciously good and his attention was entirely upon her.

"Told you already," he said. "Tomorrow my uncle aims to attend Lady B's ball, and you don't have a ball gown."

"Lady B?" She stared at him. "Lady *Beaufetheringstone?*"

"The very one."

"But . . . But . . . ." Minnie spent half of her time reading the gossip columns and the other half telling Elle, Adela, and Esme all about it. "Lady Beaufetheringstone is an important hostess."

"She's a darling," he said.

"Captain—"

"Anthony," he amended.

"I am not a member of high society. I do not belong at a high society ball."

"You will tomorrow night. Seraphina will see to it."

"But—"

"Come now," he said with a half-smile. "Isn't dressing up in a pretty gown and dancing at a ball every girl's dream?"

"Perhaps for some," Elle admitted. "But even so, a *dream.* Not reality. I know nothing about how to comport myself in a London ballroom."

"Comport?"

"The rules of etiquette. Surely you understand."

His black brows lifted. "Never gave it a thought."

"You would not have, would you? You, in your uniform littered with medals, with your face and—and—and *height* and absolute disregard for rational sense would certainly never need to know anything about the rules of society. I have no doubt that you flash that handsome smile and say ridiculously charming things, and nobody notices that you have just broken twenty rules of etiquette and mangled the English language in the meantime."

"You think my smile is handsome?"

"I have just insulted you and you did not even notice it." She turned her face to the window. "I cannot believe I am here. In this carriage. I cannot believe I spent the past two hours being fitted for a ball gown that costs more than my yearly wages. And you know very well that your smile is handsome."

"If my smile's handsome, must be a reason for it," he said so mildly she had to peek at him from the corner of her eye. A perfect example of the smile in question shaped his lips, and she knew he meant *she* was that reason.

She snapped her attention back to the window.

"Did notice the insult," he said after a moment's silence. "The compliment suited me better."

She turned her face to find him regarding her with perfect equanimity. A special little bloom of pleasure inside her felt distantly familiar and so very good.

She rolled her eyes away. "You are incorrigible," she said.

"And you'll do fine tomorrow night. A girl like you—"

"Woman."

"—with your snappy tongue and haughty nose—"

"Haughty *nose?*"

"Poking right up in the air when you're put out, just like the titled ladies of the *ton*. High society'll adore you, Elle."

"I never said you could call me that."

"Won't, if you don't like it."

But she did like it. She liked it enormously. He pronounced her name like a caress, and perhaps it was spending hours wearing a gown studded with diamonds, or all the chocolates, but she had the most pressing urge to ask him to say it again. Her name. His voice. Like a caress.

"You may," she said.

He grinned.

Of course he grinned. This was all his plan, his ridiculous lark. Not *his* future at stake. Not his real life. He could amuse himself with her troubles now and, when it was all over, be none the worse, while she would be in prison.

"If you don't want to go to the ball, Elle, you needn't. We'll find another way to replace that type," he said, entirely destroying her righteous indignation.

"You keep using that word."

"A man's bound to repeat a word every so often. Tell me which one you don't you like and I'll do my best to avoid it."

"We," she said.

His brow knit. "What other word would I use? But damned if your speech ain't finer than mine. Beg pardon— *dashed*. All right, teach me a new word, Madame Printer. I'm all prepared to expand my vocabulary."

"There is no other word for 'we', of course." Her cheeks were burning. "You . . ."

"You?"

"*You and I*. But I already told you that."

"And I remember it." He tapped his fingertip to his head and his smile broadened. "Not entirely empty up here."

He was a ship captain in the Royal Navy. Men did not win the command of vessels worth thousands of pounds, and the ruling of dozens of other men, unless they were intelligent.

"I do not dislike it when you use the word 'we,'" she finally said, too quietly probably.

"Happy to hear it." His voice was a bit rough. "You're all right with it, then. The ball tomorrow?"

"I am afraid I will embarrass you. I . . . I don't know how to dance."

His eyes widened.

"Don't look at me like that," she said, twisting her fingers together. "I never learned. I never had the time." Or the opportunity. For five years after her mother died and her father disappeared—years in which girls like Mineola, Adela, and Esme had attended country fairs and the occasional party at somebody's home—Elle had scrubbed the floors of her neighbor's house and fish shop in exchange for a pallet in the corner of the kitchen and food. Five years of raw hands and aching back and fish oil stench that would never wash away, until her grandparents appeared from America and rescued her.

"I don't give a damn if you know how to dance or not," he said.

"*Whether* I know how to dance. Then why are you gaping at me?"

"You just used a contraction. *Twice.* Didn't think it was possible." He spoke with sincerity, but the slightest crease in one of his cheeks marred the effect.

She pinched her lips to prevent a smile. "Can you never be serious, Captain?"

"Life's too full of misery, Elle," he said, abruptly sober. "No point in lingering in worries when a man can do something to make it better." He leaned forward and grasped her hand lightly. "Try not to fret, will you?" he said. "We'll work this out."

It was too much for her—his strong fingers, his wonderful scent, the honest sincerity in his gorgeous eyes. Obviously she was not as immune to scoundrels as she wished. She withdrew her hand and clasped it with her other in her lap.

"I am afraid I will not impress your uncle and that this all will have been for naught," she said. "I wish I knew how to go along at a ball. I truly do."

He leaned back against the squabs, entirely comfortable while her pulse was racing.

"Daresay you could simply stand there and look prett—" He straightened and his gaze sharpened.

"What is it?" she said.

"An excellent idea's just occurred to me. Needs refining, though. I'll have it all worked out tomorrow." His smile blinded. "Where to now, Miss Flood?"

"Brittle and Sons, please."

"Nearly dark already. I'll take you home."

"*No.*" She swallowed over the alarm in her throat. "No. Please, to the shop."

"As you wish, ma'am." His smile dimmed a bit, but he did as she wished.

~o0o~

The young curate from the charity church, Mr. Curtis, was departing when Elle entered her flat. She knew immediately the message in his gentle greeting.

"She is worse this evening, isn't she?" she whispered as she untied the ribbons of her bonnet.

"I am afraid so. I encouraged her to take some broth, but she refused. Perhaps she will do so for you."

"I should not have gone out today. With the shop closed, I should have remained at home with her while I am able. Instead I—" She dressed up like a costly doll and blushed like a ninny beneath the gaze of a naval hero. "I wasted the afternoon."

"I cannot agree, Miss Flood. You must allow yourself some pleasures, especially now. Your grandmother is happier knowing that you are happy. She informed me with great animation that you have a suitor."

"A suitor?"

"I wish you well in it," he said with a kind smile, donned his hat, and departed.

In the bedchamber, her grandmother's eyes were unusually bright.

"You are late tonight," she said in a labored whisper as Elle crossed the room. "Were you . . . with him?"

Elle's pulse beat like a little drum. "With whom, Gram?"

Her grandmother's lips crinkled into a smile. "Young Sprout told me . . . about your gentleman caller."

"The *grocer's* boy? What on earth—What stories is Sprout

inventing now? And why did you tell Mr. Curtis that I have a suitor?"

"Miss Dawson . . . called this afternoon."

"Minnie? She called here? While I was—"

"With a gentleman." Gram's papery smile widened, and quite abruptly Elle decided that she did not care if the grocer's boy or Mr. Curtis or Mineola or everybody in London knew she had spent time with a scoundrel if it gave her grandmother this pleasure.

"I was not precisely *with* him, Gram," she admitted. "He is helping me with a—well, a very important project for the shop that I must complete before Mr. Brittle and the others return from Bristol. But what did Sprout have to do with it? Did he deliver the flour and tea while Minnie was here?"

"She paid him a penny . . . to wait at the shop . . . then to come tell me." Her weary eyes were shining. "He said the carriage was glamorous."

"You don't care about carriages. You want to know about the gentleman," Elle said with certainty. "But there is nothing to tell, Gram. He is"—tall and handsome and delicious smelling and ridiculously charming and she was definitely not immune to scoundrels—"the usual sort of man, I suppose."

"Gabrielle, you are . . ." Her grandmother's chest constricted and her lips tightened momentarily. "A poor liar."

"How do you suppose that?" Elle said, hiding the lump in her throat.

"Even before today . . . I knew," she whispered, her pain so close to the surface.

"What did you know?"

"That you are happy."

Happy? Aching over her grandmother's pain, yes. Panicked over the missing type, certainly. Happy, no. Not since her grandmother had fallen ill.

"Gram—"

"Your voice . . . step . . . breaths were lighter yesterday." Her eyes were closing. "After I rest, you must . . . ." Her voice was barely audible. "Tell me about him."

But there was nothing to tell. Nothing real. This was a game to him, a momentary diversion. She had no maidenly virtue to lose; naïve fool that she had once been, she had given that eagerly to lying Jo Junior. She had nothing like that to fear from the naval captain. And her heart was incapable of making the sort of attachment to a man that she had for her grandmother and once had for her grandfather and mother. So after Elle watched her grandmother fall into sleep, she went into the kitchen and prepared dinner for herself as she did every night. That she had no appetite for it she refused to attribute to the nervous tingles that had beset her stomach for two days now. It was so much easier to blame the cakes and chocolates.

~o0o~

Again wearing his uniform, which Cob had brushed and polished, Tony drew in a long lungful of moldy air and lifted his hand to knock on the door of the miserable flat into which his former first lieutenant had moved his family after he lost everything he owned except the clothes he'd worn playing cards that night.

Mrs. Park answered it. Hollow-cheeked, with dark circles beneath her eyes and her collarbones poking through her exceedingly modest gown, she was still a fine looking woman, pretty, perhaps twenty-seven or twenty-eight—a few years older than Elle.

Adamantly putting out of his head the little print mistress, he bowed.

"Good day, ma'am."

"Do come in, Captain," Mrs. Park said softly, stepping away from the door. Everything about her except her bony frame was soft; her cottony blond hair, her pale eyes, her unsmiling lips, and her tepid voice. No spark in her eyes. No snappy color in her cheeks. No animation in her words. But of course there wouldn't be; she'd been a widow only a few days, and from what John had told him, she'd been fond enough of her husband.

"May I offer you tea?" she said limply.

"No. Thank you." He glanced over her shoulder hopefully. "Little ones about?"

"The children are napping," she said. "We walked to the cemetery this morning to visit my husband's grave. They were tired when we returned home."

The cemetery where John Park had been laid to rest was miles across town. Poor girl couldn't even afford a hackney coach to visit her dead husband.

"Glad to send a carriage the next time you wish to go," he said, a sinking sensation in his gut as he watched her dull eyes and even duller movements as she went into the sitting space of the tiny flat.

"You mustn't go to such trouble for us, Captain. You have already been tremendously generous."

Sick, sharp guilt replaced the sinking sensation.

"No trouble," he said. "My honor."

She sat on a hard wooden chair.

"Will you have a seat, Captain?" she said, gesturing, then fell silent. He'd had a number of occasions to speak with her over the five years during which her husband had served as his first officer, and she'd never been more animated than she was at this moment. By now Elle would be peppering him with queries.

Shoving Gabrielle Flood from his thoughts once again, he set his hat on the table between them.

"Mrs. Park, I've news to share with you, the sort I don't like to have to share, truth be told."

Her features remained bland. "News, Captain?"

"Your husband's gaming debts were such that he wagered his pension against them."

Alarm flickered in her eyes.

"Is that—is that legal?" she said.

He shook his head. "But there are moneylenders who'll take advantage of a man. It's one of them who holds the note on your husband's pension."

Her cheeks went white as a topsail.

"The pension was all we had," she said weakly. "I have no family, Captain. No work. Nothing. Without it . . . Oh, no. This cannot be."

"I know." He drew a deep breath. "Which is why I would like to settle your husband's debts myself. If you'll allow it."

The colorless eyes widened. "But the amount—It is not a small sum. That pension was intended to support me and my children until they are grown."

"I would consider it my honor." The devil take his useless honor. His hands were icier than the North Sea.

"You are too generous, Captain. But I cannot accept."

"I wish to do this. I hope you will allow it."

"I cannot. Why, for years already you have given my family so much. John adored sailing with you." Now her eyes watered like leaky planking, one tear dripping out after another. "When he would come home on furlough, he was always so full of tales of the *Victory* and your generosity with all of your officers and crewmen. He said you were the finest commander in the fleet, that everyone wanted to be assigned to your ship. He took such pride in working for you. Once he told me that never in his life before had he felt so useful and so appreciated as he felt serving as your lieutenant." Her damp eyes were downright starry.

"He was a fine sailor," he forced through his lips. "An exceptional first officer." *A first officer he could not have done without.* Good God, he had to end this interview. "His family don't deserve to suffer from a little gambling debt. Allow me to settle it, ma'am."

"Gambling is a sinful pursuit, Captain. As such, my husband must answer for it in the hereafter."

Good God. This, he had not expected. But now he recalled John mentioning his wife had been the daughter of some starchy vicar up in Newcastle. No wonder his lieutenant had always been eager to return to sea.

"I cannot compound that sin by accepting money from you, who are blameless," she continued fervently, driving the guilt like a dagger into his belly. "The sacred vows of marriage I spoke to my husband must make that burden mine to bear alone."

As well as her innocent children's, he wanted to point out. They seemed to be getting the short end of the stick with this theology.

"Then I'll be glad to give the money to you, and you can repay the debt yourself. Not the thing for a gently bred female to consort with moneylenders. My solicitor will assist."

"Captain," she said, lowering her eyes. "You are very generous to offer. But it would not be seemly for me to accept such a sum of money from a man who is not my relative. What would my children think when they grew to an age to understand?" She lifted her gaze again. It overflowed with sincere modesty. "What would anybody think?"

That he was a cad. A reprobate. A knave, who took advantage of a grieving woman bereft of the protection of her husband to give her a slip on the shoulder. A scoundrel who set up his former officer's widow as his mistress, whether she liked it or not. She was pretty enough to make it believable, and docile enough to make it likely with at least a third of the bachelors in the navy and a number of the married officers as well. Her religious scruples be damned, Tony knew enough of his fellow officers to be certain that, if presented with this opportunity, those other men wouldn't even give her a choice.

Tamping down the surge of panicked misery in his chest, he nodded and rose to his feet. She stood too.

"Thank you for offering, Captain. No other commanding officer would be so generous, I am certain."

He'd no doubt of that. But no other commanding officer had been such a lying, guilty wretch either.

Dropping to his knee on the bare floorboards, he shut out of his memory the last time—*the only time*—he'd been on one knee before a woman—in a printing house, with that woman's sweet, sodden foot in his hands—and said, "Mrs. Park, would you do me the honor of marrying me?"

Chapter Six

When Captain Masinter arrived, Elle was not looking out the window in anticipation. But Minnie was. And Adela. And Esme. And the grocer's eight-year-old errand boy, Sprout.

Seraphina had sent a note to the shop that morning, informing Elle that the captain would be collecting her early in the evening for the final fitting. They would all leave for the ball together, directly from her home. Elle had been unwise enough to share the news with Minnie, who shared it with their two friends. Then Sprout came by, as he often did to see if he was needed to deliver or retrieve post for Peregrine and Lady Justice, and Adela and Esme set to interrogating him on everything he had seen of the naval hero the previous evening. The four of them had swiftly become quite a merry band awaiting the captain's arrival, and Elle had retreated to the press room to suffer her agitated nerves in peace and quiet.

"Blimey!" Sprout exclaimed. "Them hacks is bang up to the nines!"

"What does that mean, Sprout?" Esme said.

"That carriage must be worth hundreds of pounds," Minnie said in hushed awe.

"Elle, he is here!" Adela whispered through the open doorway.

With exaggerated calm, Elle put away her pen, wiped her damp palms on her skirt, and went into the front room. He stood at the door, as tall, dark, handsome, and aristocratic as he had been the previous day and the day before that, smiling at her friends with undiluted good cheer.

Her stomach plummeted to her toes. She could not possibly see this through.

Then he turned his beautiful eyes to her, and his smile

changed. It dimmed, but for the better; there was no blitheness in it, only simple, sincere pleasure. He said deeply, softly, as though there were no one else in the room, "There she is."

And Elle knew she was doomed.

~o0o~

"Does this carriage also belong to Madame Étoile?" she said as he jumped up onto the box beside her and snapped the reins.

"Like it?" he said with a quick glance at her.

"The seat is so comfortable. And we are quite high off the ground, but I do not feel unsafe."

"Bought it this morning."

"*You* bought it? Today? Yesterday you said that a bachelor has no need of a carriage in town."

"I'd a mind to celebrate," he said, maneuvering the carriage away from the commercial streets.

"Oh? What are you celebrating?"

His swift smile revealed every white tooth. "Bachelorhood."

Elle did not know why the single word should make her cheeks erupt in heat, except that it was probably because she was a thorough ninny.

"Your friends were good to see you off," he said, glancing aside at her again. "Making certain I wasn't a scoundrel, were they?"

"I think they did not entirely believe that I am attending a ball tonight. *I* do not quite believe it."

"You'll be fine."

"I did not tell them about the missing type," she said, forcing her gaze away from his profile that she wanted to trace with her fingertips. "And I feel positively awful."

"Wager you did it to protect them rather than yourself."

"How do you know that?"

He only smiled.

"Perhaps it was to protect me too," she admitted.

"What did you tell them?"

"That Madame Étoile is considering hiring Brittle and Sons to print advertisements, and she wished to interview me extensively before doing so but has little time to spare."

He turned his face to her.

"I know!" she exclaimed. "I am a positively wretched liar. I could not even invent a halfway believable lie. But how could I tell them the truth? If Jo Junior even suspected that they helped me replace the missing type, he would go up and down Gracechurch Street blackening their reputations with their employers, until each of them had been released."

"Jo Junior?"

"Josiah Brittle Junior. My employer's eldest son."

"Has it in for you, does he?" he asked with a single lifted brow, and abruptly she realized that speaking to this man about her past with Jo Junior was the height of folly.

"Yes. A bit. Oh, see, we are here! So swiftly. What speedy horses you bought today, Captain," she said lamely. He knew. Casting her a curious glance, he leaped down from the box and went around the horses to assist her.

She liked the sensation of his hand taking hers. She liked it far too much. It made her feel insensibly light—almost weightless—merely his hand holding hers to assist her from the carriage. Perhaps her grandmother was right. Perhaps she was enjoying this taste of a gentleman's attention, even if it was only in order to save her position at the shop.

And perhaps she was the greatest fool alive.

Inside the house Seraphina greeted them with the same affectionate elegance as before.

"Off to change for the evening, then," the captain said as his cousin shepherded her up the stairs.

"Don't forget, Anthony. You must wear your uniform," Seraphina said and then drew Elle into the pink and cream satin room.

~o0o~

He did not wear his uniform.

Elle had a very poor opinion of sailors. Her father had been a sailor. He had abandoned her and her mother in a hovel on the unforgiving coast of southern Cornwall, to reappear after her mother's death when Elle was eight, only to sell every book and trinket in the hovel and spend it on gin then die a year later of a failed liver. She had formed her opinion of the sailorly ilk young and quite firmly.

Captain Anthony Masinter seemed cut from another sort of seafaring fabric altogether. And, however much she wished to deny it, he cut a truly splendid figure in his navy blue and whites.

Dressed for a ball, he was even handsomer.

A coat of rich blue complemented his tan skin and dark hair, and formal black breeches hugged the muscles in his legs so well that Elle was obliged to glue her attention to his face. But that proved no less taxing to her nerves. For as she descended the stairs on silk slippers and he turned from his contemplation of a painting, his beautiful eyes swept her from tip to toe, and his features went instantly, entirely slack.

"What?" she said, reaching up to cover the delicate collar of paste diamonds that Penelope had fastened about her neck and which draped over her otherwise exposed bosom. She wished she could cover up her whole body. Her shift and petticoat were tissue thin, the gown just as scant, and the overskirt entirely translucent, cinched beneath the bodice with a single silver ribbon. "Is something amiss? Am I not convincing enough?"

"As a printing-shop girl," he said in a low voice, "not really."

"As a princess, thoroughly," Seraphina said behind her. "She dresses up nicely, doesn't she, Anthony?"

"Aye." As he came forward there was a light of deviltry in his eyes that dispelled Elle's nerves and made her abruptly eager for the evening's adventure. He glanced at his cousin. "Not dressed yet, Seri?"

"I will be momentarily. But you must go ahead of me to

Lady B's. Who knows how long Uncle Frederick will last tonight? Now go fetch the carriage, Tony."

He looked about the foyer. "Your butler's broken his leg, has he?"

Seraphina chuckled lightly. "Darling, go. I must say a word to Miss Flood without you present."

"Aha. Feminine secrets." With a bow, he went.

Elle turned to the modiste. "Thank you, Seraphina. This gown, the jewelry . . . It is all perfect."

"And your coiffure," she said, scanning the smooth coils, upswept and decorated with a sparkling tiara. "Penelope is an artist with hair." She grasped Elle's gloved hand. "Now, ask me what it is you have been eager to ask me all evening."

Elle's mouth opened, but Seraphina squeezed her fingers. "Dear Elle, you have the most transparent face."

Elle looked her directly in the eye. "You and Captain Masinter are clearly very fond of each other."

"We are devoted."

"Why aren't you married? To each other. Plenty of cousins wed."

Seraphina's eyes smiled. "I was married once. My husband died several years ago."

"Did the experience sour you on marriage?"

"Not at all. He was considerably older, of course. But he was kind. No, I am not sour on marriage. And I adore Anthony. He is the best man I have ever known. But, Elle, he is not my cousin as everyone likes to pretend."

Elle felt abruptly sick. He could not have brought her to his mistress's house; it seemed so unlike him, and unlike Seraphina as well. But what else could this beautiful, independent woman be, to command the attention of such a man? From what Minnie said, men of the aristocracy took mistresses as often as men of the common class drank gin.

"He is my half-brother," Seraphina said. "From the other side of the mattress, as it were," she added with an expressive nod.

"Oh." Such relief filled her throat that she could manage

nothing more.

"You wish to know if I am acknowledged by our family," Seraphina said. "And if not, why Anthony acknowledges me."

Lips caught between her teeth, Elle nodded.

"Our father, Sir Benton, was a diplomat for many years. On one occasion while traveling in the East, he happened upon a beautiful Turkish girl. Men sometimes being what they are, he temporarily cast aside his marriage vows. When he returned to England, he forgot the Turkish girl, but nine months later my grandmother reminded him. My mother had perished bearing me, you see, and her mother brought me here to be raised in the comfort of wealth. Sir Benton's wife would not have it. She had five young sons and four young daughters of her own, and she did not like the idea of having yet another, especially not a little brown nut of an infant that was proof of her husband's infidelity. They sent me to Sir Benton's youngest aunt, a widow who had once lived abroad not far from where my mother had grown up, as it happened. Great-aunt Seraphina raised me as her own bastard, rather than as my father's." She smiled. "Thus, cousins."

"But they believe you are a cousin only?"

"Everybody knows the truth, of course. Our paths cross infrequently, though, so they rarely have reason to cut me directly."

"Captain Masinter does not cut you. He obviously cares for you."

"He protected me from them. He still does. I told you he is a good man, Gabrielle," Seraphina whispered, turning her to face the man walking toward them from the back of the house. "Be kind to him."

In the candlelight, his eyes glimmered with admiration. Elle could hardly breathe.

"Well," she said, "shall we get on with this little charade?"

He offered his arm. "My lady."

Before the house he handed her up into Seraphina's carriage, then climbed in. It was dark within, save a glimmer of light from the lamp on the street, and when the coachman cracked the whip even that light vanished.

"Don't suppose you speak any foreign languages?" he said in an unexceptional tone.

"Foreign languages? A little French. My mother was a schoolteacher before she married my father."

"Liked him that much, did you?"

This time she did not resist her smile.

"The lady's voice reveals all," he murmured.

"I am not a lady, Captain. If you fail to remember that tonight I am afraid you will be horridly disappointed when I prove myself incapable of pretending it."

"You are a lady, Elle, tonight and every night," he said in an altered tone, deeper, sending the nerves scampering back into her stomach. "But tonight you will be more than a lady."

"What do you mean?" she said warily, wishing she could see his eyes.

"Transparent as rain on a spar deck. Open your mouth tonight, and you'll blow the whole deal to shrapnel."

"Blow the— What?"

"You're far too direct, Elle. And earnest."

"I—"

"Don't take me wrong. Dashed fond of your directness. And your earnestness, truth is, it turns me inside out. But my uncle's a prize snob. Thinks everybody's a fool, and doubly so if they haven't got a title. Daresay if he knew who you really are he wouldn't give you the time of day. And, you said yourself you don't feel up to it."

"What are you saying?" she said somewhat thickly. *Her earnestness turned him inside out?* "That I have spent two days preparing for a ball I am not to attend after all?"

"No, no. Nothing like that. Just saying that you mustn't speak tonight."

"I mustn't speak? But how will I ingratiate myself to your uncle without speaking? Are you—"

"Stupid as a post? Probably. Fortunately, my uncle already thinks I've got a brain the size of a pea. Best let me do all the talking. Now, what would you like to be? Russian, perhaps?"

"What would I like to *be*?"

"Pretend to be, that is. So you needn't speak, leastways not overly much. How about Hungarian. That's it! Unlikely to be anybody who speaks Hungarian at this event. Probably."

"But what if there *is*?"

"Cross that bridge when it hatches, daresay."

Elle stared into shadow, lit occasionally by lamplight passing by outside. Arms crossed and leaning back against the squabs, he looked perfectly comfortable, like he was enjoying himself thoroughly. Teetering between dismay and hilarity, she laughed.

"There now," he said in that deep, private voice that made her feel unsteady and hot inside. "Knew it wouldn't take you long."

"You knew it would not take me long to what?"

"To fall in." Then he smiled, and she was quite certain she knew exactly how he commanded men so successfully. He was simply a big, strong, solid thing who, once determined to accomplish a task, devoted himself entirely to it. This was not a lark for him. He was doing it for her because he was exactly what his half-sister had said: a good man.

He had called her a lady, which was ridiculous. But he did not seem to understand that. He was nothing like the gentlemen who came into the shops on Gracechurch Street and made Minnie and Adela behave like cakes; not haughty or superior.

"You do not mind it?" she said.

"Mind what? Putting one over on my uncle?"

"Perilous adventure. Living on the edge of insanity."

"Not a'tall," he said. "Life's more fun when nothing's certain."

"Spoken like a man who has never woken up to an empty larder with no idea how he will eat that day."

In the striated lamplight, she saw the crease in his brow.

"True," he said. "A few tight occasions when shot ran thin and Boney's boats weren't yet all in the drink. But no starvation to speak of, thank God."

Abruptly she understood his words. She gasped. "I beg—
"

He waved it away. "I prefer a bit of uncertainty, Elle. A man can plan and strategize, stockpile cannons and gunpowder for months. But when the battle's met he's got to fly with the instinct of the moment or he's likely to be sunk."

"Not everyone has good instincts." She had not with Jo Junior.

"Spoken like a woman who don't trust hers." She felt his gaze upon her in the darkness and decided that the captain's devil-may-care exterior hid a profoundly thoughtful interior.

"A woman who *does not* trust hers," she murmured.

"Made a mistake or two based on faulty instincts, have you, Elle?"

"Borrowing the type, of course."

"Not that sort of mistake."

Of course not. The astonishing thing was that she found her lips opening and her tongue forming the word, "Once."

"Josiah Brittle Junior?" he said mildly.

"Yes. I thought I understood his intentions."

"Come to find you didn't after all?"

"No. My instincts did not prove trustworthy in that instance."

"What did he do to you, Elle?" he said in an altered voice. His eyes gleamed like opals in the darkness.

"Nothing that I did not foolishly allow. We worked together every day. I thought I knew him. I trusted him, and he took advantage of that."

"A man who preys upon a woman in his employ ain't worth the dirt on his boots."

"*Isn't.* But I was naïve. I should not have believed him." She crunched her hands together in her lap. "I have no idea why I am telling this to you."

"Because you know your instincts with me aren't wrong." He turned to look out the window and the carriage was drawing to a halt.

The Mayfair mansion of Lord and Lady

Beaufetheringstone was gigantic, with a magnificent entryway of classical proportions jammed with guests and a vast foyer full of people festooned in sparkling gowns, starched neck cloths, and priceless jewels. The ballroom was even grander, a panorama of England's most exalted elite dressed spectacularly, every one of them laughing and chatting and looking each other over.

Elle's hands shook.

"Now, Princess," the captain said and took her hand to tuck it into the crook of his arm, "let me do the talking."

~o0o~

She obeyed. At first.

"*Wallachia?*" she hissed as they moved away from the Duchess of Tarleton. "I know nothing about Wallachia."

"Neither does anybody else here," he said, feeling her fingertips pressing into his arm, her knuckles against his ribs, and in charity with the entire world. Jane Park had refused him categorically. He would find a way to help her and the little ones—help she would accept. But now he was free and the prettiest girl in the room was on his arm. "Occurred to me that Tarleton'd spent months in Russia after the war. Couldn't chance it. And foreign princesses from tiny unknown principalities are all the rage these days, don't you know."

"I know nothing of the sort," she whispered. "And I think Wallachia is actually quite a large country. Where is your uncle?"

"Just on the other side of that potted palm. Ah, here's Lady B. Ma'am," he said, sketching the matron a bow. "Outdone yourself with the festivities tonight, as always."

"Captain, who is this goddess and why haven't you brought her here before?"

"Princess Magdala of Hungary, may I present to you—"

"Ladee Bee," Elle said with a generous roll of her tongue. Bending her head gracefully, she curtsied, a single, sublime dip of her lithe body garbed in diaphanous white fabric that clung to her breasts and legs and left Tony's senses entirely muddled. Lifting her kohl-rimmed eyes to their hostess again, she said in soft, halting tones, "I am 'appy to be makeeng ov your acvaintence."

"Well, what a lovely creature you are," Lady Beaufetheringstone exclaimed, the peacock feather in her turban dancing. "Have you been introduced to the Duke of Frye? No? He spent any number of years in Bulgaria, or perhaps it was Bavaria. In any case quite near Hungary, I daresay. Come." She linked arms with Elle. "I will make you known to him. My cousin thrice removed, of course. His wife is a darling thing . . ."

The throng of people separated him from Elle and Lady B, the orchestra commenced a set, dancers crowded the floor, and he lost sight of her. Some time later he found her surrounded by guests, stumbling through English phrases with a demure and gently smiling humility that her companions obviously admired.

"Princess Magdala, everybody is simply rapt with their correspondence," one lady was saying. "He is obviously infatuated with her."

"No, no," a gentleman interrupted. "You mustn't let the countess mislead you, Princess. Lady Justice is merely playing games with Peregrine, and he is fully aware of it."

"If he knows she is playing games, my lord," another woman said, "why does he continue writing letters to her?"

"He likes to tease her."

"Dees Pere—" Elle said, her eyes innocently seeking assistance. "Pere—"

"Peregrine," a gentleman offered.

"He iz—how do you say in the Eenglish—in love vif her, yes?"

"Oh, yes, Princess!" one of the ladies gushed. "Entirely."

"He's merely flirting with her," a different gentleman said. "She has invited that nonsense by printing his letters for the public to read, after all."

"She disagrees with his politics," another said.

"Eloquent girl! Always knows precisely how to turn a phrase."

"She is the equal to any man in Parliament."

"Do you know what *I* wish?" a lady declared. "I wish I were the first person each month to read Peregrine's letters and Lady Justice's replies. Wouldn't that be splendid? Then I could tell all of my friends before anybody else heard a thing. My drawing room would be the most popular place in London."

Everybody chuckled. Elle's eyes shone and her lips were a sweet arc of delight. Across the circle, she met his gaze and a soft pink flush stole across her cheeks.

"Forgive me, ladies, gentlemen," he said, and stepped toward her. "Must steal the princess away." She nodded her coiffure regally and moved away at his side. Her fingertips pressed into his sleeve and her eyes danced.

"I spoke with your uncle," she whispered. "He is wonderfully diverting!"

"Diverting? Frederick Baldwin?" She smelled of roses or lilac or lavender. Flowers. And sugar. And perhaps lemons. Lemons with a lot of sugar in them. Amidst every perfume and cologne in the crowded ballroom, her scent was the only thing in his head and it made him thirsty. "Certain you got the right man?"

"Yes! He spoke to me in Bulgarian. Can you believe it? I hardly knew what to say."

"Nothing, I should hope!"

"Bulgarian could be similar to Hungarian, I suppose. What a disaster. How will I avoid understanding him the next time?" But she was laughing and abruptly he needed to be out of the crowded ballroom. Anywhere else. With her.

He drew her toward a doorway. "You need air."

"I do?"

"You do."

"But I was—"

"Trust me, Princess."

And she did, allowing him to guide her through the press of guests, down a corridor, and through a closed door into an empty chamber. The summer evening was warm and no fire in the hearth lit the room, only a lantern from a terrace beyond the windows illumining shelves upon shelves of—

"Books," she breathed, pulling away from him and gliding like a ghost toward a wall stacked with books from floor to ceiling. "What an absolutely magnificent library."

A library. Of all the rooms in this mansion to bring her to, he'd stumbled upon a room full of the printed word.

"Good heavens!" she exclaimed. "If I am not mistaken, this is an early edition of Thomas More's *Utopia*. Here! Sitting like any other book on an open shelf."

"You don't say?" He attempted nonchalance.

She came to him. "Look at the fine tooling of the binding. And the cut of the letters." She opened the volume and ran her fingertips along the edge of a page, stroking it like a lover. "After centuries the ink is still clear and crisp. It is simply magnificent."

"Not the only thing that's magnificent here."

Her chin snapped up, her gaze met his, and the book was forgotten.

"I—" Her gaze dipped to his mouth and her sweet lips snapped shut.

Tony smiled. "Enjoyed yourself out there, did you?"

"I wiled an invitation to tea at your uncle's house on Friday. Once he learned I was a princess, it was like taking sweets from a child." Her cheeks were flushed with roses again.

"Didn't know you had it in you, did you?"

"In truth, no. I think it is all the opulence. To be surrounded by so much beauty and wealth, and to be the only person who knows who I am, except Seraphina . . . and you . . ." She was breathing quickly now, the creamy swells of her breasts pressing against her shimmery gown. "To be playing the same sort of game of anonymity that Lady Justice plays," she said. "It has made me feel especially daring. Reckless," she added upon a whisper.

With his fingertips beneath her chin he tilted her face up. The room was dark, her eyes glittering, and he was feeling decidedly reckless himself. He couldn't resist. And he was fairly certain she didn't want him to.

Chapter Seven

In the blue of his eyes shone desire that Elle did not want to deny any longer.

"There is so little light in this room." Her voice wobbled. "I cannot see properly."

"Well, there's the lucky part of it." He drew the book from her fingers and set it aside. "You don't need to see for this."

"This?"

"This," he whispered huskily and bent his head.

It was perfect—barely touching, the sweetest, most tantalizing brushing of his lips against hers, and the stirring of every fiber of desire within her. It was poetry. It was beauty. There was quite a lot of trembling, entirely on her side.

Then it was over.

He drew back a few inches and looked into her eyes, truly into her eyes, as though he wanted to see right inside her head, into the deepest part of her brain where all the secrets hid, including the secret that she knew must not be very secret anymore since it was probably written all over her face.

And then his perfect lips curved ever so slightly and he kissed her again.

At first he kissed her carefully, as though learning her lips as he was allowing her to learn his. His lips were surprisingly soft, delicious, tasting her with one gentle exploration after another. Sweet, heady longing grew in her, an ache of need that these modest caresses fed but did not satisfy. Pressing her lips to his more fervently, she reached for more.

Upon a sound in his chest that made her entire body heat, he took her mouth entirely.

It required very little encouragement for her to open to his kiss, and even less for her to reach up to his shoulders and cling there. His hand cupped her face, then he was coaxing her lips apart, drinking kisses from her lips and then—*oh heaven*—her tongue. He kissed her again and again, his mouth hot and hungry and beautiful and she never wanted it to end. Hands surrounding her face, he sought something in her mouth that she most definitely wanted to give, bending to her deeper, more completely with each meeting. His tongue swept hers and she moaned and twined her fingers in his hair and surrendered herself thoroughly to him.

He broke the kiss.

With an involuntary chirp of protest, she opened her eyes. His were dark and more astonished than she liked.

Air jerked out of her lungs.

Dropping his hands from her face, he reached for her wrists and removed her arms from his shoulders. Then he released her and stepped back. He was blinking now and he shook his head once.

"Didn't you—" She took a deep breath and tried to steady her voice. "You did not enjoy that, I guess."

"Good God, Elle. If I'd enjoyed that for a minute longer I would now be enjoying all of you on that divan there."

She choked on the flare of heat that coursed straight up the center of her body.

"That—That suits me." She folded her hands before her.

His beautiful mouth cracked into a grin. "You look like a princess and you taste like a goddess. But you still sound like a little print mistress."

"Thank you. I think?"

"Thank you, most certainly." He ran his hand distractedly through his hair—his hair that she now knew felt like satin and wanted to feel quite a lot more.

It must have shown in her eyes. His chest heaved upon a hard breath.

"We've got to get out of here, now," he said, "before I do something I shouldn't."

She wished he would. But she appreciated the wisdom in his suggestion. Being discovered in this manner would not help her achieve her ultimate goal. A bishop of the Church of England was unlikely to welcome a wanton hussy into his house for tea.

But with Captain Masinter's gaze upon her now, Elle did not feel wanton or hussy-like. She felt beautiful.

Going to the bookshelf and replacing the *Utopia*, she moved to the door. From behind, his hands circled her shoulders, big and strong and astonishingly gentle and he bent his head and kissed her shoulder. Her entire body shimmered in pleasure and a sigh slipped through her lips. Lightly he ran his fingertips down her arms, and stroked his thumbs over her palms. She shuddered and tilted her head.

"I could stand here all night tasting you, yet never get my fill," he murmured against her shoulder. "Wonder what those blokes in your native country call it when they feel this way."

"My native country?" she whispered.

"Hungary." His lips brushed her earlobe and pleasure cascaded all down her side. "When they feel this ravenous for a girl"—his teeth grazed her neck and she gasped at the pleasure—"d'you suppose they say they're English? You know, 'By Jove, I'm devilishly English for that pretty girl!'"

She giggled. Then she cleared her throat. "Not girl. Woman."

The lightest caress of his lips feathered over her skin. "I am devilishly hungry for you, woman."

His mouth was doing remarkable things to her, but his hold on her hands remained loose.

"You're not slapping my face," he said, his voice muffled behind her ear. "That's a good sign."

"How is that a good sign?" she said unsteadily.

He laced their fingers together, her small palms against his, and a little moan escaped her.

"You don't think I'm a scoundrel now," he said.

She drew her hands away and moved the final step to open the door.

"I do still think you are a scoundrel, Captain." She knew better than to lose her wits over provocative words. "It is only that I do not mind it quite as much as before."

~o0o~

The captain collected his half-sister and they left the Mayfair mansion and drove across town to the printing house.

"Now," he said as the carriage halted before Brittle & Sons, "you'll tell me where you live and we'll see you home. Properly."

"I cannot."

"Have you a grand secret you are unwilling to divulge, Elle?" Seraphina said. "Perhaps you truly are a princess, and only playing at being a printer's assistant. Is that it?"

"I cannot explain, but I cannot allow you to see me home."

"Then you will come home with me and sleep in my guest bedchamber," Seraphina said, taking her hand, "and tomorrow morning after we have had a cozy breakfast and talked over every detail of the grand success of Princess Magdala of Hungary tonight, my coachman will return you here."

"Thank you, but I cannot. I have work to do in the morning." And Minnie sitting at her grandmother's bedside waiting for her return.

"Elle," the beauty said, "it is already the morning."

"You have been so kind. Please forgive me." She squeezed Seraphina's hand and tugged hers free. She turned to the captain. "Thank—"

"No. What sort of man do you imagine I am, to leave a woman in the middle of the night to walk home along deserted streets?"

The sort she had kissed before. The sort that, after taking her virginity in the press room and telling her she would "eventually get it right," went for a pint at the King's Barrel and left her to clean up shop for the evening.

But he was not now looking at her like that sort of man.

"The streets are not precisely deserted," she said, feeling peculiarly shaky. "The King's Barrel is still full of patrons. And

I have walked along these streets late at night any number of times."

"Not in that rig, you haven't." He glanced at her gown.

Her hands darted to the forgotten tiara and necklace. Unclasping them, she passed them to Seraphina.

"With all due respect, Seraphina," she said, "if being a lady means having one's freedoms curtailed, I am glad not to be one."

"Hm." Seraphina slid the paste jewels through her fingers. "I think with that statement, you have effectively ruined my brother's night."

"She hasn't," he said.

"Oh, see!" Elle said, panic crawling into her throat. "There is Mr. Curtis, the curate from the church. He is probably on his way to visit parishioners in my building."

"After midnight?"

"I will engage him to walk home with me." She reached for the door handle.

He covered her hand with his and leaned forward. "*He* knows where you live?"

"I am quite well acquainted with him, in fact. Please, Captain."

He turned the handle. Before she could descend, he climbed out and strode to the curate and introduced himself.

"I am pleased to meet you, Captain," Mr. Curtis said. "I will be glad to escort Miss Flood to her building, certainly. I suspect her grandmother will be eager to hear how the evening went."

"Her grandmother," he said, turning his gaze to her. "Yes, of course."

As Elle walked away beside Mr. Curtis, Captain Masinter remained in the street behind them, tall and rigid and solid, watching her go. It was for the best. Kissing a man did not mean she must allow him into her life. Her world. Her reality that had nothing to do with balls and aristocrats and victorious naval captains.

Rather, quite the opposite.

~o0o~

"Why have you come here?"

"Well, that's a fine 'good day.'" Blocking the press room doorway, with a silk hat lodged beneath his arm, the captain was better looking than ever in an exceedingly well-tailored coat, neat trousers, and boots so highly polished Elle might have checked her coiffure in them. But she never checked her coiffure, most especially not this afternoon when she had not expected to see anybody all day. Dressed in her shabbiest ink-stained gown, she looked a thorough fright.

"Always thrilled when a lady demands to know why I'm calling. Instantly reveals how happy she is to see me," he drawled but his gaze was as warm as on the night before when he kissed her.

At the ungodly hour at which she had finally fallen into bed, she had vowed to put that kiss out of her mind entirely.

Kiss.

Kisses.

Now his lips slipped into a half-smile and she snapped her gaze up to his eyes. Good heavens, she really must take care not to stare at his mouth.

"I am happy to see you," she said and instantly regretted it when his smile widened. "But I did not expect it," she hurried to add. "Tea with the bishop is tomorrow, of course, and today I am involved in a project—"

He stepped forward and bent his head toward hers, and Elle's tongue forgot how to make words.

Close to her brow, far too close, he said, "And what project might that be?"

"After all those people at the ball went on and on about Lady Justice and Peregrine, I had an idea." She felt dizzy. She tried to catch her breath, but it would not catch and she suspected it was because he had consumed all of the oxygen in the room like he was consuming every ounce of her calm. She willed her hands to be steady as she spread out the broadsheets that lay on her desk. "Everyone in London is enamored of their correspondence. Everyone in Britain, really. Mr. Brittle has saved all of the broadsheets—"

"Mr. Brittle saved them? Or Miss Flood?"

"Yes," she admitted. "I enjoy rereading them. And . . ."

"And?"

"My grandmother loves hearing them read aloud."

"Ah, yes. The top-secret grandmother who is well known to trustworthy Mr. Curtis."

"She says their correspondence reminds her of my grandfather's courtship when he was young and too proud to admit his love directly." A smile tugged at her lips. "Early in their acquaintance she suspected that he was smitten with her, even though he waited quite a while to declare himself. Until then she had great fun reading between the lines of his teasing remarks to decipher his affections."

"Your grandmother is an admirer of Peregrine too?"

"And Lady Justice. Like so many people! Which is how this idea occurred to me. What if Brittle and Sons were to compile the best letters and pamphlets of Peregrine and Lady Justice, and publish them in a single volume?"

"A single volume? What for?"

"For entertainment. For posterity. For every society hostess who wishes she were the repository of all things fashionable. We could bind it in fine leather and give it a marvelous title, and sell it for twenty times the price for which the broadsheets themselves sold originally."

"Miss Flood, you have a shockingly material appreciation for your hero and heroine's love affair."

"Oh, well, the decorative binding and the price are for Mr. Brittle's sake. He would never take to the idea if he did not believe he could turn a profit from it."

"Turning a profit is not your purpose, then?"

"I would simply like to see their letters collected. At least my favorites."

"Which are they?"

"These." She passed her fingertips over the pages. "These are the most heartfelt."

"Sounds like a capital idea, Elle." His voice seemed sincere, but not entirely like him either.

She looked up into his face, but he was staring at the broadsheets, a thoughtful frown creasing his brow beneath a lock of glossy black hair. She had touched that. She had touched him. Now, if she wished, she could reach up and touch him again. She could lean onto the desk and put her lips beneath his, and feel his kiss again. And perhaps taste his jaw too. The muscles there were bunched. She wanted to run her fingertips and then her lips over them and loosen the strain there.

Abruptly he turned his gaze to hers and she choked on her own desire.

She slapped a palm over her hacking mouth.

"Quite all right there?" he said in a low voice.

"Yes." She coughed again. "Yes, that is—*yes*. The Brittles will return from Bristol in a sennight, and I hoped to have a proposal for the volume on Mr. Brittle's desk when he arrives. Therefore, you see, I really must finish this—"

"Not this afternoon." He drew the pen from between her fingers. "This afternoon you are coming with me."

"To where?" Damn her wretched voice for quavering. And damn her heart for wanting him to reply, *To a dark room so I can kiss you silly again.*

As though he knew her thoughts, he smiled a smile that sent her swift heartbeats into her toes. Then he set the pen in its stand.

"To meet my sister at the shops," he said, backing away. "Aha, didn't expect me to say that, did you? Miss Flood, I might very well be a scoundrel, but I'm not such a scoundrel as all that." With a decidedly rakish grin, he went into the front room and called back, "Come along. Madame Étoile awaits her live doll."

As he handed her up into his dashing carriage behind the matched grays, she said, "Live doll?"

"Can't call on my uncle for tea in rags suited to a ball."

"Rags?"

"A mantua," he said, snapping the reins. "Pinafore. Whatever the blazes females call it."

"A gown?"

He scowled. She had never seen him scowl. Other men scowled, even on occasion mild Charlie and pacific Mr. Curtis. Not Captain Masinter. He was the most blithely untroubled man she had ever met, the sort of man who might kiss a woman in a dark library until she was a puddle and think nothing of it. And yet he was a naval captain, hardly an untroubled profession.

But she did not want to care whether he scowled or not, or why. She did not want to care about him in any manner. And she most certainly did not want to long for more of his kisses, no matter how the sight of his strong hands on the reins made her insides flutter rather aggressively.

"The gown I wore last night is beautiful. It will do for tea." She could hear the acerbic tone of her voice and did nothing to soften it. Instead she took refuge in Lady Justice's frequent critique. "The aristocracy wastes a ridiculous amount of money and time on superficialities. Only look at this carriage."

"You said you liked this carriage."

"And that coat"—the coat that displayed his shoulders to gorgeous advantage—"must have cost a fortune, when—"

The gaze he turned upon her was full of pleasure. And *affection*. Undeniable affection.

Elle's breath went entirely out of her.

"Stop looking at me like that," she managed. "I was chastising you."

"Rather be chastised by you, Gabrielle Flood, than praised by anybody else."

"Then you are very silly."

His forehead crunched anew. "No doubt of that."

"All right, I will ask. Why are you scowling?"

"A grandmother." He pulled the carriage to a sudden halt.

"A *grandmother*."

"What are you doing?" She looked around at the traffic. "You cannot stop driving in the middle of a busy street like this."

"I'm a decorated hero of the Bombardment of Algiers and a member of the Order of the Garter. I can jolly well do anything I like. You live with a *grandmother* yet you never mentioned her to me?"

"Why should I have mentioned her to you? I hardly know you."

His eyes blazed and he looked directly at her lips. "Is that so?"

He had a point.

"I met you only five days ago," she spluttered.

"Thought you were a stickler for precision."

"I am a stickler for precision. But I have no idea why you are noting that now."

"We met seven days ago," he said.

"You knocked me over seven days ago. You spoke to me like a human being only five days ago."

He grew abruptly somber. "I'm sorry I didn't apologize to you for that, Elle."

"You did apologize. Begrudgingly, perhaps. But you did."

"I was in something of a hurry right then."

"Were you?"

He paused, then said, "My first officer had a spot of rum luck that day. Extraordinarily rum luck."

"And you were rushing to him with a bottle of brandy?"

"I was rushing to his wife to collect her. Wanted her to be able to pay her last respects before he died."

Her eyes and lips flew wide.

"Oh, Anthony," she said. "I am so very sorry. I had no idea."

"Couldn't have." He grasped her hand. Her fingers felt perfect in his, lithe and beautiful. "Now say my name again."

"W-What?"

"You just called me Anthony."

She snatched her hand away. "You are incorrigible."

"And you're repeating yourself. That's a good sign." He looped the reins and jumped off the box. His visit to Jane

Park's house that morning had dispirited him. She was no closer to accepting a gift of money than she'd been two days earlier. But the little ones were hungry as the devil. They had gobbled up the cakes and fallen upon the game of Spillikins he'd brought like ravenous dogs. The widow had tried to reject the gifts, but blast if he would let her pride and religious scruples keep those children sunk in misery. He would find a way to make her accept charity. He had to.

Rounding the team to the other side of the carriage, he extended his hand to Elle and the tangle of frustration in his chest eased.

"Of what is *this* a good sign?" she said as she descended. "That you are an incorrigible scoundrel?"

"That I fluster you," he said.

She tugged her fingers away again. "You do not fluster me, Captain."

But he did. And it filled him with the most extraordinary sensation. She wanted him. At thirty-four he was seasoned enough to recognize desire in a woman's eyes. And she had kissed him as though she wanted him. No shrinking virgin here.

But she did not trust him. That was as clear as rain in a barrel.

"If you insist, Miss Flood." He leaned close and took a long pull of her intoxicating scent. "But I'll have you know, I am an experienced tactician. Trained to notice these things."

Alarm skittered across her features.

Exiting a shop nearby, Seraphina waved and Elle moved swiftly away.

Blast his cursed tongue. Instead of distressing her he wanted be making those eyes sparkle, making her laugh. She deserved it. She deserved happiness. And he was determined to see that she got it.

With renewed resolve, he went after her.

Chapter Eight

Seraphina greeted her warmly and drew her into a shop.

"It is an absolute delight to have the opportunity to poke about in shops, Elle. Look at this lace. It is far too expensive for the quality. But that lace there is divine. Now, watch as I inspect these closely," she whispered. "The shopkeeper will peer at me suspiciously until I reveal my name and then he will fall all over himself. So will those matrons over there, who will eavesdrop until they are able to insert themselves into the conversation."

It happened exactly as she predicted. When Seraphina drew her into the conversation, the shopkeeper and ladies barely glanced at her stained gown before fawning over her too.

She enjoyed it far too much, she suspected. The captain, however, shared only a few charming remarks with the matrons. When Seraphina asked him to cross the street to perform an errand for her, he went without a word.

"What have you done to my brother, Elle?" Seraphina asked a quarter of an hour later as he came through traffic toward them again. "I have rarely seen him so subdued."

"I have done nothing." The notion that she *could* do something to disturb his equanimity was ludicrous. Yet the night before, after their kiss, he had obviously been shaken. "Is he subdued?"

"Most assuredly."

"It's done," he said as he met them on the footpath. "Where to next, ladies?"

Seraphina's attention shifted past his shoulder to a man and a woman nearing. They were dressed expensively if somewhat severely, and their faces were grave.

"Good day, Mrs. Starling," the man said, making a shallow bow to Seraphina. He sniffed. "Anthony."

"How d'you do, George? Alice." The captain's smile did not reach his eyes.

"We are well," Alice said. Ignoring Seraphina, her gaze briefly alighted upon Elle then returned to him. "Will you attend Sir Benton's birthday celebration a fortnight hence, Anthony?"

"Both me and Seraphina, of course. Wouldn't miss it. Looking forward to seeing all the little ones. By the by, how's James taken to university? Making top marks?"

"Of course," George replied. "But we expect that, naturally."

Seraphina said, "George, Alice, may I present to—"

"Must be moving on then," the captain cut in. "Elsewhere we've got to be. George, Alice, always a pleasure." He turned to her and Seraphina. "Ladies?" With a decisive nod, he gestured them toward another shop.

When they were inside, Seraphina turned upon him.

"Why didn't you introduce Gabrielle?" she whispered.

He glanced out the window, impatience stamped on his features.

"Couldn't stand the idea of it, if you must know," he said, then faced Elle. "Terribly sorry. Absolutely beastly of me," he said, but it was as though he were reciting an apology rather than giving it freely. It was the first time she had ever heard him speak without sincerity, and it made her feel ill.

"Well, then," he said quickly, his voice a strange, discomposed growl, "I'm sure you don't need me here." He gestured to the cases displaying ladies' gloves and reticules. "And, great guns, there's Nik Acton on the street. Haven't seen him in an age. Ladies." Sketching a quick bow, he went out of the shop.

"Elle, I beg your pardon," Seraphina said. "He is not himself. Something preys upon him, more than George and Alice."

"You needn't apologize." Perhaps he truly was unhappy that she had never spoken to him of her grandmother. But that was preposterous. Why would such a man care about that? "I am not insulted. I understand that socializing at the ball was to a purpose. I do not expect you and the captain to introduce me to all of your friends now."

"But of course we will! Dear Elle, you have it the wrong way around. I suspect that Anthony hurried us away because he wished to spare *you* from knowing *them*."

Her eyes popped wide. "But, who were they?"

Seraphina's generous lips twisted. "Our eldest brother and his wife."

Elle had no siblings of her own, but Minnie and Adela were fond of theirs. Even Jo Junior and Charlie, for all that they were different sorts of men, shared a bond.

"They were so . . ."

"Cold? Snobbish? Rude?" Seraphina supplied.

"Why did he—George—call you Mrs. Starling?"

"It is my married name."

"Ah." *Étoile* meant star, of course. "How wonderful that you have a pseudonym."

"Just as your friend Lady Justice." Seraphina smiled and took her arm companionably to leave the shop.

But Elle's pleasure in the outing would not return so easily. "Alice ignored you."

"Alice always snubs me in public," Seraphina said lightly. "She is practicing for when George succeeds to the baronetcy and she will cut me entirely. Their sense of superiority is enormous. All of them, not only George and Alice."

"On what grounds? Your father's title?"

"Oh, no." She paused before a shop window full of trinkets. "Upon the grounds of their own intellectual eminence."

"Intellectual eminence?"

"My half-siblings include a mathematician, two physicists, a master of ancient history, a theologian, and a patroness of a literary society. If you wonder how growing up as a cousin to those excessively superior individuals was, imagine growing up as their brother."

"But the captain seems to like everyone."

"He is unlike them, Elle. And they have always been unkind to him. Even now they poke fun at his profession, as though he is playing at toy soldiers." She turned away from the window and her eyes lit. "Here he is returned."

He was not alone. With him now were a tall, slender woman hand-in-hand with a tiny blond girl, a man whose golden good looks were godly, and a girl just on the verge of womanhood. On the captain's shoulders perched a miniature brunette, her palms spread over his eyes.

"Is this her, Uncle Anthony?" the tiny blonde said, and all of their eyes came to Elle.

He peeled one little hand from atop his eye and smiled so beautifully that Elle lost her breath.

"Aye, Letty. This is her. *She*." He lifted a brow. "Right?"

"Correct," she barely whispered.

"Miss Flood," he said, "may I make you known to her ladyship, the Countess of Bedwyr?"

"Since you are a friend of Anthony's, I beg you to call me Jacqueline," the countess said. Her accent was foreign, soft, and almost shy. "This is my husband and his ward, Claire. And these are my daughters, Letitia and Margaret."

"How do you do, Miss Flood?" The Earl of Bedwyr bowed gorgeously. "Madame Étoile, a pleasure, as always."

Elle was gaping. Among Brittle & Sons's most popular publications, a poem published in three parts titled *The Stone Princess* had seen enormous success. Demand for the poem continued so high for so many months that Mr. Brittle had finally compiled the parts into a bound volume. It was the very book that gave Elle confidence he might do the same with Lady Justice and Peregrine's letters.

Here before her now, as gloriously handsome as the faery prince in the poem, stood the anonymous author of *The Stone Princess*.

"I proof-corrected your poem at Brittle and Sons!" fell out

of her mouth. "Oh, I beg your pardon, my lord," she mumbled, her cheeks burning. "I am mortified that I just said that."

Lord Bedwyr grinned. "I am now especially honored to make your acquaintance, Miss Flood. And I am grateful for your assistance with that project. Now, you must tell us where you had the misfortune to meet this fellow." He gestured to the captain.

"At Brittle and Sons, course," the captain said.

"A printing house, Anthony?" the earl said with a skeptical twist of his lips. "You?"

"Horse threw a shoe just in front of the shop door, don't you know," the captain said breezily. "Had to fix the thing long enough to ride home. Went inside to beg the loan of a tool. Isn't that so, Miss Flood?"

She did not trust her voice. She nodded.

He was keeping her secret. And he was looking at her again in that manner he had of making her feel that no one else existed except the two of them, as he had looked at her in the library.

"Then a horse's lost shoe is clearly to our advantage," Lady Bedwyr said with a smile at Elle.

"Mama!" the miniature brunette exclaimed, then abruptly draped herself over the captain's head and whispered into his ear. He nodded, and she peered at her mother. "Uncle Anthony wishes to take us to eat lemon ices," she declared.

"And?" he whispered up to her.

"And he says that if you do not allow it, his heart will break and he will set out to sea again this instant in order to mend it!"

"Lemon ices it shall be, then," Lady Bedwyr said. "For we must not lose the captain to the sea again so soon."

~oOo~

His entire bearing changed. As the girls ate ices and the rest of them took tea, he was again liberal with his smiles. Unlike his brother and sister-in-law, these friends were warm and affectionate with Seraphina, and they extended their warmth to her as well. They were obviously his real family. Elle sat mute in her shabby gown, which none of them seemed to note, mingled pleasure and astonishment paralyzing her tongue, and her heart grew thick with longing.

Once upon a time, she had known this deep affection, before Grandfather died. Then Gram's health collapsed. After that there was mostly pain and quiet endurance, and occasional happy minutes when they read Lady Justice's pamphlets.

She should now be home with her grandmother, not shopping for lace and gloves that she would wear once and taking tea with beautiful, wealthy people who would not remember her tomorrow.

Abruptly the captain stood up and went to the counter. When he returned he came to her side.

"Miss Flood," he said quietly, "if you wish me to convey you anywhere at this time, I am at your command."

"Said as prettily as an opera singer, Anthony," Lord Bedwyr murmured.

"Stubble it, Charles," the captain said without removing his attention from her. Then his gaze dipped to her lap, where her fingers had twisted a serviette into knots.

"Do you wish to go now?" he said.

It was yet an hour before she typically left the shop. Mr. Curtis would soon be calling upon her grandmother. She could return home early and relieve him of that duty.

She looked into the sailor's eyes, at the tiny crinkle lines radiating from the corners that revealed a life of both enormous responsibility and much laughter, and she shook her head.

"Not yet, please," she said.

A half-smile cut his mouth. "Knew you couldn't resist spending more time with me."

"You are a regular Romeo, Anthony," the earl drawled. "It is a wonder Miss Flood can withstand your roguish charm for even a moment."

"Isn't it?" Grabbing a chair from another table, the

captain plunked it down backward between her and Lord Bedwyr, and settled himself on it, his muscular thigh not an inch from her knees. "Now, Miss Flood, tell us all a nice long tale about the barrels of errors you found in my friend's poem here. If there weren't many, invent 'em. Longer the story, the better."

"Why? To embarrass Lord Bedwyr?"

"Not at all. Don't think he's capable of embarrassment anyway. I simply like to hear words come from your lips. Watch them too. Best show in town."

At that moment it was fortunate that they were in a public place and surrounded by people. For if they were not, she had the most dreadful certainty that she would swiftly be making speech impossible for both of them.

Chapter Nine

Bishop Baldwin lived on a quiet avenue in an austerely elegant house filled to the brim with every conceivable valuable item that a man of means might consider worth having. There were clocks and snuffboxes and ancient swords and decorative lanterns and crystal vases and lamps, a pair of oars signed by Admiral Horatio Nelson and a punting championship cup, three chess sets of blown glass, marble and wood, boxes and small caskets of all sorts, jewelry, two flutes, a brass trumpet, a worthy cello with its graceful bow, several exotic drums, three spectacular masks of the sort one saw in parades, a gilded birdcage in which a mechanical bird repeatedly pecked at a dish, a collection of beautiful quill pens, another collection of peacock feathers that burst from a sturdy Roman amphora tucked in a corner, oil paintings and watercolors and maps occupying every inch of the walls, a dish of rare coins, a string of Catholic rosary beads fashioned entirely of lapis lazuli, a number of interesting chairs, thick rugs of Eastern design in every room, and one suit of medieval armor.

Most of the objects were arranged on tables and windowsills, while some rested on floors and others hung from the ceiling. All were easily accessible to a person wishing to examine them.

The only item about which Elle truly cared was locked in a glass case.

"What's this, Uncle?" the captain said, tapping his fingertips on the top of the case casually, as though he and she had not been throwing each other exasperated glances for an hour during which they drank tea, Elle pretended to be a Hungarian princess, and the bishop told them about every item in his collection except the Warburg chase.

"Ha!" the bishop exclaimed. "Never thought you'd care about that, my boy."

For an instant, the captain's fingertips ceased tapping. Then they started up again.

"Daresay," he said. "Let's open up this thing and see it, what?"

A gold watch chain stretched across the bishop's waistcoat. Now he tugged on it and withdrew not a watch but a key that he fit into the lock on the glass case.

"Go ahead," he said to his nephew. "Lift it out of there, boy."

The sinews of the captain's big, strong hands strained around the frame packed closely with type and Elle got instantly light-headed.

"Good God, Uncle Frederick, it weighs more than *Victory*'s anchor."

"That, my boy, is no peas-and-pie lump of iron. That is part of a Warburg printing press, built in seventeen fifty-five. There are only six of 'em in existence today. One of 'em, Your Highness, is right here in London at a shabby little printing shop, sad to say. I imagine they don't even know what they've got."

"Mm," she murmured, struggling not to guffaw, her nerves flying.

"Let her highness get a good close look at it, boy."

That the bishop called this grown man "boy"—this victorious commander of a naval vessel whose hands she was imagining wrapped around *her* rather than around the chase—made a giggle well up in Elle's throat. That he was inviting her to stand beside that so-called boy, arms touching and heads bent, so that she could smell his cologne and pick out every detail of the tiny scar on his chin and hear his breathing, made her want to shout thanks to the bishop and tell him to leave the room at once.

Then he actually did.

"I'll go tell my man to bring up the Mesopotamian steele,"

he said, shuffling toward the doorway. "I keep that one in storage, of course. Ever since that thieving footman stole my enameled Egyptian box a few years ago, I've kept the most valuable foreign pieces under lock and key. Like that German printing press there. No, no, you go ahead, Princess! Enjoy it," he said, waving a knobby hand. "Ain't very often it comes out of the case."

"*Isn't,*" the captain murmured and slanted her a wide smile. A lock of hair dangled over one eye and he looked indeed boyish and as giddy as she felt.

"Set it down," she whispered, "so that we can both pick out the pieces. It will go more swiftly."

"Better pick them all out yourself. Ensure it's done right."

"Oh no! I didn't think—Did you bring a container?"

"S'why a man has pockets in his waistcoat, Your Highness."

She reached into the frame. "So he can steal printer's type?"

"And whatever other items appeal, of course. Quickly now."

Pulling out two slips of metal, she let her hand hover near his coat.

"Now don't get missish on me," he said. "We've got a task to accomplish here."

Brushing the front of his coat aside, she found the waistcoat pocket. When her fingers met the silky fabric and the hard body beneath, she nearly fumbled the type. Cheeks burning, she managed to deposit them in the pocket. She repeated the action several more times before he spoke.

"Have you got the missing pieces memorized?" His voice was unusually rough.

"I thought it best, given our need for haste." She slipped another two into the pocket, allowing her fingertips to linger on him. "But I think I had already memorized them out of sheer guilt and dread anyway."

"You are extraordinary," he said so close she felt the words stir her hair.

"Twelve, thirteen," she counted as she dropped two more into his pocket. "Because I am guilty and filled with dread, or because I can memorize fifty-three pieces when it is my task every day to read hundreds and hundreds of them?"

"Yes," he said as though the word came from his chest. Elle had never felt quite so hot in her life, except perhaps in the library when he had been kissing her.

She glanced up at his face.

So close.

Such intensely blue eyes.

And his mouth. *His mouth...*

"Clement's bringing up that tablet now." The bishop's creaky voice sounded in the foyer.

Elle pushed the type together to fill the tiny holes in the frame and backed away from the captain.

"Shouldn't need more than a few minutes to find it." Bishop Baldwin shuffled back into the room. "Had enough of the Warburg, have you, Your Highness? But it's true, females ain't got the head for machinery, even royal females. Put that in the case, nephew, and I'll lock it up."

The captain did as bidden. Elle's stomach twined with panic as Bishop Baldwin tucked the key into his pocket. Beckoning her toward the stone tablet that his butler carried into the room, he launched into a dissertation on its inscriptions.

The captain extracted them from the house, then, with fantastic efficiency.

"Well, that is that," she said as he snapped the reins.

His face was set in stern lines.

"Daresay," he said firmly.

Her stomach was in knots of equal parts panic over the remaining forty missing pieces of type and distress over the finale of their quest. He had done what he could to help her. Now his part in the ruin she had made of her life was over. He would drop her at Brittle & Sons, turn the stolen type over to her, and drive away to be charming and handsome and delicious with some other woman.

"Thank you for making the attempt."

"Thought it'd turn out better," he said upon a frown.

"I am sorry you went to the trouble of it all."

"No trouble." He sounded sincere, but the frown lingered. "I hope you will give Seraphina my thanks, and tell her I will return the gowns to her tomorrow." She fingered the pleats of the gown the modiste had loaned her to take tea with the bishop, silk exactly the color of the captain's eyes. "She has been very generous."

"She's a good girl." He cut her a quick glance. *"Woman."*

Perhaps this had not all been a waste. At least if this one member of the elite began to understand Lady Justice's message of equality between people, even between the sexes, something good had come of it. Ensconced in her prison cell, Elle would find comfort in that.

"No choice now," he said and his voice sounded different. A hint of a smile creased his cheek.

"No choice?" she said.

The smile became a full-blown grin. "We'll have to break in."

~o0o~

"I repeat, this is a mistake," she said as Tony pulled the curricle into the mews and jumped down from the box. Not waiting for him to go around, she slid her perfectly curved behind onto the driver's seat and extended a hand for him to take. He grasped her waist and lifted her down.

She pulled away swiftly and made a show of smoothing out her skirt. To hide her pink cheeks, he suspected.

Today she wore the same dress from tea with his uncle the day before. But whatever she wore, simply looking at her made him hot, hard, and desperate to put his hands on her. When she had been fiddling with his waistcoat, her hands that had been plenty eager on him in the library were tentative to the point of maddening. He had nearly dropped the box and done what he really wanted to do, what he'd wanted to do again for days.

She, however, was keeping her distance. Markedly so. Despite her blushes—and those questing hands at the ball— she clearly didn't want any part of him now. Since he was not in fact a scoundrel, he had to respect that.

He didn't have to like it.

"Not a mistake," he whispered, taking her hand and drawing her to the rear entrance of the house. Pulling a key from his pocket, he fit it in the lock.

"Where did you get that?" she exclaimed.

"Shh." He laid his forefinger atop her intoxicating lips. "I stole it from Clement before we left yesterday."

"The butler?" Her eyes were perfectly round, her lashes like starbursts. "You *stole* it?"

"When he gave me my hat. Out of his pocket." He drew her inside and left the door ajar behind them. "Done it a hundred times before. Since I was in shortpants."

"I am beginning to understand how you were so blithe yesterday about this theft," she whispered as he led her along the cool basement corridor past the kitchen and butler's pantry, to the stairs. "You should have been a pirate, or at the very least a privateer."

"Considered it," he said quietly, peering up the stairwell. Evening was falling and there were no lights above yet and her hand was snug in his and all was well. "Dashed fond of the naval uniform."

"You are wonderfully profound, Captain," she said dryly.

He looked down into her face to which he was developing an addiction. "And honorable."

"Are we going up, or shall we just stand here in the dark all night discussing your penchant for theft?"

"I'm game for standing here in the dark all night if you are. Or standing anywhere else in the dark with you, for that matter."

She tugged her hand free and slipped around him to mount the steps. He followed, considering how she might respond to him wrapping his hands around her hips and pressing his mouth to the small of her back. Probably *not well*.

Once on the ground floor she went on silent feet to the drawing room that was swiftly sinking into darkness. On the floor above, his uncle was sound asleep. For at least thirty years, Bishop Baldwin had bedded down at half past seven each evening, and his servants either hared out for the night or hid away in their quarters above. It was already eight o'clock. They were in the clear.

Halting before the glass case, she turned her face to him. The silvery light of the summer evening splashed across her skin, and he wanted her like he'd never wanted a woman before—from the back of his throat to the balls of his feet and everywhere in between. Everywhere.

"Did you steal the key to this too?" she whispered.

Slipping a rigging knife from his pocket, he snapped the lock open. The sound echoed through the room, along with her little gasp of delight. Lifting the case's lid, she plucked type from the container.

Tonight she had taken care to bring a sack with her—no more accidental caresses at his waist—and she stuffed it into his hand. It filled swiftly, heavier as each piece of type fell into the sack with a soft *chink*.

"Nephew? *Princess?*" The crackly voice came from the doorway. "What in the devil are you doing to my Warburg?"

Her moan of defeat nearly unmanned Tony. Setting down the sack he turned to his uncle. But she spoke first.

"I am sorry, my lord," she said shakily. "So very sorry."

"What's happened to your voice?" the bishop demanded. "What in the devil is going on here, boy? So help me, if you've filched so much as a mote of dust from this house, I'll see you thrown off your ship and out of the navy as quick as you can say Blackbeard's wooden leg."

"Already out, sir," he noted. "But that's neither here nor there at present, of course. I—"

She moved forward. "It is not his fault, my lord. It is entirely mine. You see—"

"Uncle Frederick." Tony stepped in front of her. "She's about to try to take the blame, but it's not hers. She'll say, 'Me and the scoundrel—"

"The scoundrel *and I*," she muttered.

"—hatched an elaborate plot to rob you of an item in this case."

"There's only one item in that case, you nincompoop: my Warburg!"

"But she didn't. It was my idea, and I dragged her along into it. So if anybody's to be strung from a yardarm it should be me."

His uncle peered across the dim room. "Are you a Hungarian princess?"

"No. Forgive me, my lord."

"Ha! Put one over on everybody at Lady B's, did you? Hm. Well, my holy orders oblige me to forgive you, missy, so you've got my forgiveness. But you're a fool to hang about with my nephew, and that's the truth of it. Never known a more thoroughly addle-brained ninny in all my life."

"Laying it on a bit thick there, Uncle, what?"

"Get out! Both of you!" He waved his spindly arms about. "And don't you darken my door again, boy. Odd's bod, my sister should've drowned you in the river at birth. We'd all be better off for it."

In the foyer, the butler was holding the door wide open for them.

"Clement, you fool," the bishop shouted. "How did they get into this house today? Did you let him steal your key again? Out of here, I say! Out, now!"

She did not take his arm to descend the steps to the street, and she walked beside him to the mews in silence. In the past his uncle's hysterics had always made excellent entertainment. But the grave mask of her face now made all of that rot.

"I cannot believe what he said to you," she said, finally breaking the silence. Beside the carriage, she looked up at him. "I cannot believe it."

He shrugged. "He's said worse. They all have."

"Your family?" Lantern light revealed the astonishment on her features.

"Listen to you, worrying about a bit of name-calling when I've failed you with that dashed type. I'm sorry, Elle."

Her brow pleated, and she turned to the carriage and climbed up onto the seat without his assistance. They drove in silence. He felt like a mainmast had fallen over on top of his ribs.

"We'll devise another solution," he said.

"Stop saying that."

"Saying what exactly?"

"We."

"*I'll* devise another solution."

"No, you will not. I will. Alone. This is not your responsibility, Captain."

"Damn well is."

"A gentleman should not say such words in a woman's hearing."

"A gentleman can say whatever he likes, whenever he likes, and to whoever he likes if the occasion warrants it."

"*Whomever*," she said quietly. "But I do not believe that is your sincere conviction," she said quietly.

"Damn well is at present. Why won't you let me help you, Elle?"

"You have helped more than necessary. Thank you for it. But I would like you to drive me to the shop now."

"Is it because I bungled it tonight? Don't trust me to make it right, do you?"

"No. I appreciate what you have done. Very much. No one—" She turned her face away, giving him a view of the molasses silk he'd had against his cheek three nights ago. By God, she felt good, and smelled good, and he had to make this right for her.

"No one else would have gone to the extent that you have," she said after a moment. "You can feel perfectly comfortable leaving it to me now."

"That's a tub of barnacles, and you know it. I won't—

what did you say?—*feel perfectly comfortable* abandoning you to this now, not comfortable at all."

"You have no choice in the matter," she said firmly.

"I damn well do. It's half my fault and I'll see this through, devil take it."

"Captain," she said, "I must ask you to respect my wishes—"

"While you disregard mine, is that it? Listen here, Miss Flood, a naval officer worth his salt don't retreat from a battle—"

"*Does not* retreat from a battle."

His chest filled with the most insane warmth. "Does not retreat from a battle," he repeated. "He breaks out every gun on deck and pounds away at the enemy whether he's got a clear shot or not."

"Captain, while I appreciate the military metaphor—"

"*Analogy.*"

Her eyes snapped wide. He wanted to laugh. He wanted to grab her up and kiss her rosy cheeks and pink lips and make her sigh.

"While I appreciate the military analogy you have offered," she said, setting her jaw like an adorable little mule, "with all due respect this situation is not a firefight, and—" She looked past him and then her head swiveled around. "Where are we? This is not Gracechurch Street. I do not recognize this neighborhood."

He pulled the carriage to a halt along a row of houses on the street lined with flowering trees, and leaped off the box. A boy came and took the horses' leads.

"Where are we?" she said as Tony came around to her side.

"My house."

"*No.*" She gripped the sides of the seat. "Drive me home. Please. This instant."

"Please and this instant? Undecided whether to request or demand, are you?" He offered his hand.

"Captain Masinter—"

"Anthony." He smiled.

"You must take me home. *Now*."

"I don't know where your home is. You don't trust me enough to tell me, though God knows I haven't given you reason not to."

A man and woman walking along the footpath stared at them. Tony bowed.

"Evening," he said pleasantly, then to Elle: "You're making a scene."

"I am not making a scene, but if I were it would be entirely your fault."

He extended his hand again. "Come inside and you can berate me while I find something for us to eat. I'm famished. You must be too."

"Captain—"

"Oh, look, another of my neighbors out for a stroll. Think I'll just invite—"

She climbed down and went up the steps and into his house with gratifying haste until the door closed and she rounded on him.

"What do you think you are doing, forcing me to enter your house? A bachelor's house? At night, no less!"

"Nobody saw," he said, "except the woman next door poking her nose through a crevice in her draperies. And the stable boy. And—"

Her hands flew upward and covered her face and her shoulders shook.

"How many servants do you have?" she mumbled through the cracks between her fingers. He had the damnedest sense that she wasn't crying; rather, struggling not to laugh.

"Two. You've met Cob. He'll be somewhere upstairs now, doing whatever it is he does now that he's got a house instead of a ship to keep in order."

Her fingers slid down to reveal her sweet eyes. "Mr. Cob served on the *Victory* with you?"

"Cabin steward and all-around mother hen. You had an ally in him tonight, by the by. He didn't like the idea of breaking into my uncle's house either."

"He is a reasonable man, obviously."

"My cook's on furlough for the week. But I'm not entirely useless in the kitchen. Miss Flood," he said with abrupt formality, and extended his arm. "Care to join me in the stateroom for dinner?"

Elle bit back the hilarity lapping at her—hilarity borne of equal parts horrible dread over her future and her need to not let this end—and walked past him to the stairs.

He was in fact far from useless in the kitchen. She offered help but he declined, bidding her sit at the table with a glass of wine and wait. As he prepared dinner with swift efficiency, she watched him and had the dangerous thought that she would like to watch him like this forever.

"How did you learn to cook?"

"Cook-room of a revictualling ship," he said, arranging two plates and setting one before her. "Two years." He offered a fork and her fingers brushed his as she accepted it. When he spoke again, his voice was lower. "Three years in the cook-room of the next ship. Nearly got trapped there." He sat across from her and took up his glass of wine.

"I can understand that! This is absolutely delicious." She looked up and nearly choked on the mouthful. He was not eating or drinking, but leaning back in his chair, arms loosely crossed, half-lidded eyes intent upon her. She scooped another forkful. "How, then, did you escape a future as a ship's cook?"

"Bought an officer's bunk." He cocked a half-smile. "Some advantages to being a son of a baronet, even a fifth son."

"I should think there are many advantages," she said, wiping her lips with a towel. "But son of a baronet or not, you cannot purchase your way into commanding a ship of the line."

"Can't you?"

"You excel at your profession, Captain."

"If you say so," he murmured. "Finished?"

"Yes. Thank you. You have not eaten so I suspect that you pretended your hunger to make an excuse to cook for me."

"Did I?"

"And I admit that I was in need of dinner. My situation seems less hopeless now, though I am not at all certain how I will wrest free of this trouble."

"You won't," he said. "We will." He came to his feet and went to the door.

She reached for her plate. "I should—"

"Elle," he said with the deviltry in his eyes that made her feel delectably light. "Baronet's son. War hero. I cook. I don't clean."

She followed him up the stairs and into a chamber furnished with masculine accents: wood-paneled walls, a modest writing table, and a comfortable leather-covered chair arranged across from a sofa before the unlit hearth.

Her gaze got stuck on the sofa. And every thought, wish, and fantasy of kissing him crashed into her imagination at once.

She could feel him watching her. Her eyes sought something else—anything else—anything *safe*. It found a large bound volume lying open atop the writing table.

"Oh! This is a captain's log, is it not? I have heard of such books, of course. But I have never actually seen one. You are the first ship captain—"

Then he was beside her, shutting the book and standing far too close.

"—I have ever met," she finished haltingly. "May I see it?"

"Only a draft," he said, taking it up and shelving it behind the desk.

"I should like to see it, nevertheless. You know, of course, about my interest in books."

"This one's got nothing interesting in it." He stood with his broad shoulders blocking the shelf. "Day after day of clear horizons, endless skies, sailors bored to pieces. Dull as caulking."

"You misunderstand," she said with a smile, reaching around him. "It is not the content that interests me so much as the format." She plucked it out again and opened it. She studied a page, then flipped it and studied another. "I had no idea captain's logbooks underwent rewriting and editing in this manner. I always assumed they were like diaries. Is this sailors' shorthand that you employed in haste, and this"—she pointed—"the text that you rewrote when you had more time? Or perhaps this part is secret code. How thrilling!"

"No."

She glanced up. His handsome face was stony.

"*Oh.*" She closed the book and reshelved it. "I beg your pardon. I never meant to pry into naval secrets."

"No secrets in that log. Nothing anybody can't read," he said stiffly.

"Then I apologize for—well—for—I don't know. What have I done?"

"Nothing. You've done nothing wrong." For an extended moment he simply looked down into her eyes. Then he pulled out the logbook again and opened it. "This"—he pointed to the rows of neat, carefully penned sentences—"was written by my first lieutenant." His voice was tight. "And this"—he pointed to the shorthand—"I wrote."

"I see," she said hesitantly.

"You don't," he said. "It's not shorthand or code. It's nonsense."

"Nonsense?"

"Look."

She studied the writing. The hand was firm. But it was not indeed shorthand. It was English—barely. Words were misspelled, even transposed with each other. Other words were missing or simply wrong, and letters were occasionally scribed backward, like the letters on type. Slowly she made sense of the prose, just as the transcription did in the margin above each line.

"I do not understand," she said.

"That makes two of us." His gaze was on the page. "Madness of it is, sometimes I can't even read what I've written."

Her heart was beating so hard she could hear it in the

stillness.

"Did you never learn—that is, did you not study?"

"Endless school, Elle. When that didn't take, tutors who plied the stick again and again, trying to force a decent sentence from my pen. Boy can speak, ergo he should read and write. Truth was, I could barely speak. Mixed up words, sounds. Couldn't read my lessons. Couldn't read time from the face of a clock. Couldn't even say what was left or right. Devil of it was, nobody'd acknowledge it. None of 'em wanted to admit the Masinter family had produced a bona fide idiot. Except Seraphina. She tried to help. Number of her books I ruined, throwing them at walls . . . Finally got myself out of there. Ran to the closest port. Signed on to a ship."

"You ran away from home? When?"

"New Year's Day, seventeen ninety-nine."

"But—You could not have been—"

"Twelve."

A gasp escaped her.

"Plenty of war makes plenty of work at sea, Elle."

For a moment her throat was too tight to allow speech. She traced the edge of the ship's log with her fingertip.

"You succeeded," she finally said.

"Battle opens up the ranks quick. The Admiralty needs men with experience during wartime."

"I mean that you succeeded in making yourself understood." With such casual panache, carelessly to the point of charm. But perhaps not *actually* careless. "Your usual speech, the incorrect grammar, it is not sailor's cant as I assumed, or even fashionable insouciance, I think," she said. "You have cultivated that speech to deflect attention from actual mistakes that you might accidentally make. Haven't you?"

He did not respond. She looked up and saw in his eyes the truth of her words.

"In fact you succeeded enormously," she said. "How did you do it?"

"Hundreds of hours on my knees swabbing decks, daresay. Makes a man desperate to improve himself."

"Captain."

He blew out a voluble breath. "Picked up tricks here and there. Navigator on my first cruise was a capital fellow, shared a few ideas. Passenger on my second cruise happened to be a linguist. Said he'd known a boy like me in Ireland, two more in Wales. He was glad to work his experiments again. And I'd time. Plenty of it. Most days at sea are hours and hours of nothing. I would've been an even greater idiot not to have succeeded, at least some."

"You are trying to lessen your accomplishments. That isn't right. You should be proud. You should shout it out to the world that you were able to overcome this impairment."

He lifted his hands, his strong, calloused palms facing up, and Elle abruptly needed air. She was probably falling in love with his hands. It was positively ridiculous, but there it was. Then he tugged the cuffs of his shirtsleeves out from his coat. Embroidered into each cuff was a tiny block letter, on the left a P, and on the right an S.

"Port," he said, spreading the fingers of his left hand. "Starboard." His right hand stretched wide. "Cob started sewing them in years ago. The old salt said it'd be better to cheat than to mistake it during battle." He chuckled, then shook his head. "I haven't overcome it, Elle. Just found ways of getting around it."

"That is what everyone does when beset with challenges."

"You don't. You don't lie."

"I lied to a bishop today!"

"I lied to everyone for years."

"No one knew?"

"Cob. And my first lieutenant." He gestured to the logbook. "And now you."

"*No* one else?"

"Bedwyr. And Westfall, commander I served under during the war." His head was bent. "Seraphina, of course. The rest of our family, too, but they don't think a naval officer needs to know how to read and write anyway." The pleasure returned to his eyes. "Truth of it is, half of the time, he don't."

"Doesn't." With a gasp, she bit her lips.

He laughed softly. Then his face grew sober again. "Are you disgusted?"

"Why would I be? Because the hero of the Bombardment of Algiers does not always dot his I's and cross his T's?"

"Bit more than that."

"I am not disgusted, Captain." He had overcome this to succeed. It gave her hope that miracles were possible. "Far from it."

"If the Admiralty knew, they wouldn't have given me a command."

"Then it is a very good thing for Britain that the Admiralty did not know."

"You're not angry?"

"I have just said—"

"Angry that an illiterate fool can climb to the top of the ranks while you, clever, articulate, are trapped in the back room of a shop working for men who don't appreciate you."

Clever. Articulate.

"I do not feel trapped. With each of Lady Justice's pamphlets that crosses my table I am doing a service to the people of England."

"You deserve better, Elle. You should be publishing pamphlets of your own, or books or what have you, not correcting others' work."

"I want to slap you for saying that."

"For saying that?" He grinned. "Among everything I've said to you . . . and done?" The intensity returned to his gaze that now strafed the shoulder he had kissed the night of the ball.

"No one has ever called me clever before." Her tongue had a will of its own. "Or articulate."

"'Bout time they begin. Everybody. Friends, acquaintances, passersby on the street. You deserve it."

Her lips twitched. "Passersby?"

"I'll put an ad in the paper. Every soul who publicly declares you clever and articulate gets a guinea and a pint of ale."

"You will bribe strangers to compliment me?"

"Whatever it requires."

"Whatever it requires to accomplish what?"

"Whatever it requires to wipe the care from those pretty eyes forever."

They stared at each other. An astonishing, powerful pulse seemed to course between them. Her heart pounded.

She snapped the logbook shut, shoved it onto the shelf, and moved across the room. Away from him. Away from temptation. Away from certain misery. Miracles did *not* happen every day, at least not to her. She refused to voluntarily compound her misfortune.

"If you will be so kind as to convey me to Brittle and Sons, Captain, I will be much obliged."

"Can't do that," he said, remaining where he stood. "We've got the matter of fifty-three pieces of type to replace in the next four days. Rather, forty now."

"No, *we* do not."

"Yes, *we* do."

"Captain—"

"Anthony."

"Captain—"

"Call me captain once more, woman, and I'll—"

"You will what? Keelhaul me? Or make me walk the plank?"

He crossed his big, muscular arms over his chest. "Been considering it."

"Which?"

"Yes, you are a witch. But I don't hold it against you."

"That was *which*, as in—"

He chuckled.

Her teeth clamped together.

"You are so prim at times," he said with such obvious affection that it wrapped around her and made her feel warm and safe and good. "Can't resist teasing."

"You are a scoundrel."

"You say that so often I'm starting to think you wish I were," he said in an abruptly deep voice. And then he smiled a smile that set off an explosion of heat inside her.

As if he knew what was happening in her body, his eyes changed.

She bolted for the door.

"By *God*, you're difficult," he said behind her.

"Fortunately for you, you need not contend with my difficultness any longer."

"Difficultness isn't a word."

"Oh, look who's Captain Vocabulary now. It most certainly *is* a word and—"

"You set every inch of every surface of my skin on fire."

She spun around to him. He was breathing hard, his chest rising and falling jerkily.

"W-What does that mean?" she said.

"You feel it too."

No, no, no. "F-Feel what?"

"You're stuttering. At the ball you kissed me."

"*You* kissed *me*."

"You kissed me back, and you've been pretending it didn't happen, but it did." He searched her eyes. "Don't try to tell me this is only me."

"Only *I*," she whispered.

"What's holding you back, Elle?"

Their vast disparity of rank. Her wary heart. Everything except the way she felt when she was with him.

"I want to go now," she said upon a note of urgency.

For another long moment they stood entirely still, staring at each other as uncertainty crackled between them. Then he broke the paralysis, passing her by and moving toward the door.

Elle turned to follow. He swung around, grabbed her shoulders, and captured her mouth beneath his.

Chapter Ten

It was neither a short kiss nor a tentative kiss, nor really just one kiss. It was long, intoxicating, hungry, and it went on and on. Air was not necessary, only lips touching, caressing, needing, and hands finding shoulders, cheeks. His fingers speared through her hair, holding her to him as he consumed her lips. Her hands delved beneath his coat and spread over his chest, and he groaned and sought her deeper. They kissed and she wanted it to never end, to fly away to a place where this was everything, everything in the world here in his mouth, his hands.

Which was insanity beyond insanity.

She pushed him away. "I *cannot* kiss you. I—I must go."

"Good idea." He raked his hand through his hair and she ached with wanting to do it for him. "You shouldn't be here," he said. "In a bachelor's house. What in the devil are you doing here?"

"What am I—You brought me here! You *made* me come inside."

"Out of my mind. I was *out of my mind*. Good God." He ushered her toward the front door, and even the brush of his fingers upon her lower back made tendrils of heat slip all through her.

"You—" She looked up over her shoulder. "You are making me *go* now?"

"Yes." The syllable was hurried. He paused and looked down at her, and alarm ricocheted through her. His eyes were bright, fevered. His perfect lips parted. "Unless you—"

"I *do not*."

"Course you don't." His voice was gravelly. He pivoted

again toward the door.

"What are—I—" Words would not form. "You—"

"What? I—"

"Why are you limping?"

"Not quite limping," he said, somewhat strained.

"Then what—"

"A man can't—that is, don't like to say—I've—*Miss Flood*," he snapped, as if he were on the deck of a ship, but huskily. "*Go*. Now."

She drank in his profile and the rush of heat inside her was so astonishingly good. Her feet would not move. The next statement popped out of her mouth without her approval.

"I don't want to go."

"You *don't* want to go?" He shook his head. "No. No. I'm certain you do. And I want you to go too. I'll call Cob down. He'll drive you home." He opened the door, stepped back from it, and turned his face away. "If you please."

"I want you to kiss me again," she whispered.

His eyes shut and the gorgeous sinews on his fists bulged. "I pray you, madam."

"Please kiss me again," she said.

"Gabrielle—"

"Captain, *kiss me*."

He slammed the door shut, seized her shoulders, and pulled her against him. "Certain?" he said over her lips.

"So certain that I wish it were already happening."

It was more than a kiss. It was ravishment, pure and simple, although who exactly did the ravishing to whom was not in the least bit clear. His hands were all over her—on her back and arms and neck and her back again—but hers were all over him too. When he kissed her throat and tugged her earlobe between his teeth she allowed it. Indeed, she whimpered her approval and spread her hands on his chest, then slipped them down his waist to his sides, making herself drunk on the hard contours of his body. He was so male, so muscular, so perfectly formed and she needed to touch every part of him.

Then her breasts were in his hands. She didn't know quite how it happened. But she encouraged it. It was the height of weakness to allow it, but it felt so good, so very good, the gentle cupping of his big strong hands and then—upon her gasp— the touch of his fingertips, the stroking, fondling, caressing her nipples to a madness of pleasure.

"You are beautiful, Elle. Your face. Your hands. Your body. Your breasts," he uttered, his lips on her neck making her wild. "Beautiful. Perfect. Every part of you. Every inch of skin I've glimpsed and every curve I've only seen clothed."

"I cannot breathe."

"Dratted stays," he murmured against her neck. "Let me help with that."

He unfastened the hooks of her gown with remarkable speed. It gaped open at the back.

"What are you doing?"

"Helping you breathe." Where he tugged down her gown and undergarments his lips found her bare shoulder. Pleasure rushed through her.

"This is *not* helping me breathe."

His hands were inside her dress now, moving down her back, his fingertips descending on either side of her spine, pressing inward, feeling her, memorizing her shape. Explosions of pleasure deep inside her followed his caress.

Clearing the stays, his palms spread over her lower back. Then lower.

She gasped.

His hands stilled. His breathing was hard.

"No farther, I promise," he said roughly by her ear.

"*Yes* farther." She reached back, covered his hand with hers, and pushed it down to her buttock. They both groaned and he took her mouth with his again. His palm was large and wonderful. Given his hand's position of leverage, it seemed the most natural thing in the world next for him to draw her hips gently against his. And then not so gently. And then tightly.

Thigh to thigh, with his arousal hard against her, Elle shuddered.

"You feel good," he said very roughly. "Like heaven."

"So do you."

Hand on her neck, then in her hair, then encompassing her jaw and tilting her face up, he kissed her, pulling her in and exploring her at once. She loved having him inside her, his tongue making love to hers, and his fingers around her behind. Clutching his sleeves, she felt his thigh come between hers and moaned when he urged the muscle against her. Trapping her hips between his thigh and his hand, he made her ride him. She sought breath; this mimicked mating better than anything she had felt, ever. And he was giving it to her, making her feel him, making her insane for more.

Then, suddenly, his hand was between them, between her legs, *on her,* touching her through her skirts. Air hitched in her throat. He stroked and the sweetest, hottest sensations tripped through her. Wild need collected. So swiftly, she throbbed. The ache was sublime, his caresses a mastery of restraint and encouragement at once, exactly what she wanted. Needed. Desperately, *desperately.* She rocked her hips, bearing down on him. She had never imagined this pleasure. Never *this.*

He groaned and his fingers went deeper. "Sweet Elle," he whispered. "Whatever you do now"—he captured her lower lip with his teeth—"*don't* lift your skirts."

That was all it required. Everything burst, her pent breaths, her trapped moan, and the coiled pleasure under his hand. Cascading in shudders of heat, it seized her body, making her cling to him and cry out as he urged her through it.

When the final, stuttering sigh escaped her lips, he took her face between his palms and kissed her. She wrapped her arms around his neck, feeling him with her whole body pressed to his and the hunger in his kiss.

"Shouldn't have let that happen," he said, his lips barely leaving hers to utter the words.

"This is—"

He held her mouth to his.

"This is a—" she tried anew, but he took her lips again, then again. She loved his mouth, his kisses, how he gave and took at once. She could kiss him forever.

"This is a moment," she finally managed to say upon laughter, "when if you used a pronoun I would comprehend where I stand much more clearly."

He lifted his head only enough to look bemusedly into her face. "You're standing in my arms in my house. Rather, in my foyer, good God."

She was smiling too widely. But she had never felt like this, like a hot, sated rag doll who could nevertheless lift off the ground at any moment and fly.

"*Who* should not have let that happen?" she said.

"*I* shouldn't have let it happen, of course," he said, his hands still surrounding her face, his arms still framing her shoulders, and the rest of his body making no indication that it intended to release her from entrapment against the wall any time soon. "You'll never trust me again." The intensity of distress in his eyes stole her breath.

She slid one hand inside his coat and felt all the taut muscle of him.

"You did not let it happen," she said. "You made it happen, as you make everything happen that you want. For it, I am grateful."

A decidedly roguish smile curved his lips. "Are you?"

She licked her tender lips and nodded. His gaze locked on her mouth and everything inside her got weak with fresh heat. His Adam's apple rose and fell sharply.

"You've got to go," he said deeply. "Out of my house. Now. Immediately."

"That would probably be best."

Swiftly he buttoned her gown as she straightened her hair, then he guided her outside with haste.

~o0o~

She allowed him to drive her home, but she did not invite him to enter the building. Before the door, he took her hand and lifted it to his lips. The soft kiss made her want to sing.

The curate's young wife had visited this evening, as she did once a week when Mr. Brittle required Elle to stay late at the shop. Tonight she had lit a candle in Gram's room. It was beeswax, brought from the church so she could read aloud to Gram. Mrs. Curtis had left it because she knew Elle could not afford sweet, clean beeswax. She could barely afford tallow.

Blowing out the flame, Elle swallowed back the thickness in her throat. There was such kindness in the world. Without it, she and her grandmother would not have survived even until now.

"Were you . . . at the . . . shop?" her grandmother rasped.

"No, Gram." She wrapped her hand around her grandmother's fragile fingers. So little life crept through these limbs now. The sickness had wasted her, slowly, cruelly. That there could be in the same reality her grandmother like this and a strong, big, muscular man so full of life seemed utterly impossible. "Tonight I was—"

"With him." Her grandmother's whisper smiled.

"I kissed him. That is, he kissed me. Well, we kissed each other." And touched and exploded in pleasure. *She* exploded. He exhibited heroic restraint.

"Tell me about him."

"He likes to smile. And laugh. He is kind. Affectionate. And honorable." When he wasn't robbing a Prince of the Church. "He is a ship captain, Gram. Or he was until recently. An actual war hero."

"He sounds wonderful."

"He might be." He was. Perfectly flawed and perfectly wonderful. "The other night, Gram, you said you thought I was happy. And I think it's true. I am happy. But the most extraordinary thing is, I feel . . ."

"What do you feel?"

"Innocent." Despite the kisses, and touches, and everything that she should not have done with him. "Jo Junior made me feel so dirty. So wrong." As though simply caring for him were somehow her error. "But this, with him, it feels innocent." It felt beautiful. "He makes me laugh, and he cares about people. He is such a good man." Fear climbed up her throat. She laid her cheek down on the coverlet, facing away from her grandmother who always seemed to see through her. "Gram. I . . . I am . . ."

"Afraid of losing this happiness."

Then Elle's breathing stalled as her grandmother's frail hand stroked her hair.

It had been *so long*. So long without caresses. No wonder she had fallen apart at his touch.

"I know you wonder why I have not yet brought him here to meet you."

"Yes."

"I cannot, Gram." Her voice trembled. "When he goes away as he inevitably will, I cannot have the memories of him in this house." Memories of his smiles and his laughter in these rooms. "I could not bear it."

"You are strong, Gabrielle," came the whisper in the darkness. "Stronger than you realize."

Elle lifted her head. But her grandmother was already asleep.

~o0o~

Elle did not want to greet the new day—a day in which her grandmother was fading away and forty pieces of type were still missing—with a smile. But she could not help it. Smiles bubbled up her throat and onto her lips, refusing to be harnessed.

Bathing her grandmother, and then coaxing her to take a cup of tea and a spoonful of porridge, she kissed her and walked the three blocks to the shop. When she passed the spot where she had dropped the chase, she did a little pirouette.

Unlocking the shop door, she removed her bonnet, tossed her umbrella into the stand, and went to her worktable with a springy step. He had promised to call at lunchtime. He said he had an idea he would pursue in the morning, and then together they would contrive a solution to the missing type. She could not imagine what solution, but she trusted him—she trusted his outrageous daring and his determination—and she was willing to make the effort if it meant seeing him again. A solution must occur before the Brittles returned from Bristol in four days. It *would.*

When at half-past ten the door opened in the front office, she set down her pen and slid off her stool. Minnie's employer never allowed her to leave the shop in the morning, but Esme or Adela sometimes managed to steal away for a quick cup of tea. Or it could be the captain—*early*—as eager to see her as she was to see him.

It was not Esme or Adela or the captain or even a customer. By the front door, Mr. Charles Brittle was folding his umbrella and removing his overcoat, and Elle knew that her briefly shining lucky star had abruptly set.

Chapter Eleven

"Good day, Gabrielle." With sandy hair and hazel eyes, Charlie was an uninspired version of his elder brother's blond gorgeousness. He did the shop's books and wrote contracts and in general was not particularly interesting. She had no idea how a man like this could make Esme's pulse flutter, and it bothered her that while her friend was so obviously infatuated with him he had never once looked at Esme.

Now he seemed to assess the flush rising to Elle's cheeks and her tightly clasped hands.

"How have you been?" he said.

"Very well." *A big fat lie.* Except today. Today she had been extraordinary. Until this moment. "How did you enjoy Bristol?"

"It's crowded at this time of year, of course, and you know how I despise the sea." He moved toward her. "But Mother seemed pleased, and Hattie, of course." He always said Mrs. Josiah Brittle Junior's name flatly. Like Elle, Charlie had never taken to his brother's wife.

His gaze traveled about the office.

"Won't you ask why I have cut my holiday short, Gabrielle?"

"Yes. Naturally, I am curious." And *dying.* Unlike Jo Junior, whose interest in the family's business was all about money and social connections, Charlie actually cared about printing. Because of it, they were friends. He shared her passion, even if he did not share it with any *actual* passion.

"I had a letter yesterday, Gabrielle, from Abel Pickett."

"Oh?" The apothecary across Gracechurch Street could not possibly know about the missing type.

"He wrote to me because he is fond of you and did not wish to plunge you into trouble with Father. He said you have been transacting business in our absence."

"I have not. I would never disobey your father's orders." *In that manner.* "I never have."

"That was my thought. You are not a liar."

Elle could do nothing but stare. And wait.

"Mr. Pickett gave me details of the"—he shifted from one foot to the other—"the customer he has witnessed enter the shop several times in the past sennight. From what he said, it seems to me, Gabrielle, that this man is probably not in fact a potential client."

"What man?" She forced her voice not to shake.

Charlie came forward and took her clasped hands into his own.

"You are an honest person and, despite my brother's wickedness, still wonderfully naïve."

Considerably less honest and naïve than he believed.

She drew her hands away. "What do you wish to say to me?"

"You and I have our differences on occasion. But I believe you know that I care about you."

Impatience prickled up her neck. She could not bear another moment waiting for the axe to fall.

"Charlie, please, speak directly."

"Mr. Pickett said your caller is a gentleman, a man of attractive appearance and costly attire. He said he believes the man is a"—his eyes recoiled a bit—"a naval officer."

Charlie hated the sea.

Elle squared her shoulders. "Yes. I admit it. An acquaintance, a naval officer, has called here several times this week. How that is Mr. Pickett's concern, however, I cannot fathom."

"Gabrielle, men like that, men who can have any woman that appeals to them at the flick of a wrist, they are not—" He drew himself up. "They are not honorable men." His gaze grew surprisingly firm. "They chew up women like you and spit them out without a second thought."

She gaped. And every tiny niggling worry she had harbored about Captain Masinter's intentions came roaring back.

"Has he called on you at home?" Charlie said. "Has your grandmother met him? Or does he only waltz through here while you are alone, unprotected, when he knows you are vulnerable?"

Charlie's concerns were entirely reasonable, of course. But last night in the captain's house, she had not felt vulnerable. She had felt powerful. Beautiful. *Cared for.* As no one had cared for her in years.

"I see," Charlie said. "He has not met your grandmother. Either you are ashamed to tell her about this flirtation with a man you do not actually respect or he has made excuses not to meet her."

"That is not—"

"I don't like it that a man of that sort is calling on you, Gabrielle. I don't like it and I will not stand for it."

"You will not stand for it?" She backed away from him. "Charles Brittle, you have no right to tell me whom I may or may not see. If I wish to consort with—"

"Consort with?"

"—a handsome war hero—"

"*War* hero?"

"—I very well will."

"Gabrielle—"

"That is, no, I have not been consorting with him." Only briefly at a ball, then in his foyer. *Not nearly enough.* "We have been working together on an important project."

"A project? Is that what he calls taking advantage of a lonely girl? By all that's holy, Gabrielle, do you hear yourself? A fortnight ago you were a modest, disciplined, hardworking, sensible girl. Now you are a—"

"Woman." The captain stood in the open doorway, his jaw rigid, his bearing decidedly military, and his gorgeous blue eyes spearing Charlie like a fish. Abruptly Elle could think of nothing except that he had arrived early after all.

"She is a modest, hardworking, disciplined, sensible woman," he said to Charlie. Then he turned his gaze upon her. He bowed. "Miss Flood, how do you do?"

Better. So much better.

"Captain," she said, "this is my employer, Charles Brittle. Charlie, this is Captain Masinter."

The captain nodded.

Charlie bristled, but said, "Good day, sir," between his teeth. "You have happened upon a private conversation between Miss Flood and I. I wonder if you wouldn't mind stepping outside until we have finished."

"I would mind. Miss Flood, are you at liberty to allow me to take you up in my carriage?" He spoke slowly, articulating each syllable with sober authority, and Elle realized that when he spoke formally it was always thus. Now she understood the reason for it. The effort it must cost him to make no mistakes would be enormous, and the anxiety he must feel— recognizing that he would not even know if he did make a mistake—must be terrible. She wanted to throw her arms around him and tell him that he was more than a war hero; he was simply a hero.

"I should like to convey you to call upon my sister," he continued. "She has awaited your visit for several days now."

"Sister." Charlie snorted. "Likely story."

"Charlie," Elle snapped. "You are being ridiculous."

"No, Gabrielle, I am not. I understand the nature of men much better than you do, and I—"

"I advise you, Mr. Brittle," the captain said, "to reconsider your words before you continue speaking. Or, ideally, to simply cease speaking entirely."

With each word, he was making her want more fervently to drag him into the press room and ravish him on the spot. Her heart was bursting.

"I will not cease speaking," Charlie said. "You have been carrying on a secret flirtation with Miss Flood here in this shop, that any number of our neighbors have witnessed."

"If the neighbors have witnessed it," the captain commented in his wonderful, easy voice, "how do you suppose it's secret?"

Charlie's jaw flexed. "Twist my words. But I will not sit back and allow this to continue. You, sir—"

"Captain." A feral warning smoldered in his gaze fixed firmly on Charlie's face, and a shiver of heat went straight from Elle's lips all the way to her belly, to fan out in the most decadently wicked manner between her thighs.

"Captain Libertine, I've no doubt," Charlie spluttered. "Why, he probably has a woman waiting for him in every port, Gabrielle. Don't you, *Captain?*"

"Not at all," he said, and his gaze slid to her. Deviltry glimmered in it. "I've at least two or three per port."

"Captain," she said with a smile she could not restrain. "You mustn't tease Charlie. He will think—"

A woman walked through the open shop door behind him.

Casting the captain a glare, Charlie went forward. "Good day, ma'am. How may I help you?"

"Good day," she said softly. "I am searching for—Oh, here he is. How lucky."

The captain's features went slack. He turned his shoulder, looked at the newcomer, and Elle actually saw his chest compress in a sudden exhale.

"Captain," the woman practically sighed, her face a pale oval of genteel feminine loveliness. "I am so happy to find you finally. You cannot imagine what a search I have had."

"The little ones," he said abruptly. "Are they all right?"

"Little ones?" Charlie said.

"The children are as well as can be expected," she said. "They would be glad to see you."

The captain inhaled thickly, his shoulders falling.

"Intended to call upon them—you all—this afternoon," he said.

Charlie's face was livid. Elle's stomach churned. She grappled for the doorjamb behind her, found it, and gripped it until its edges bit into her palms. There was cotton in her ears, and a whooshing sound, like the rustling of the branches of trees beset by storm winds.

"You must wonder how I have come to find you here," the woman said sweetly. She was *all* sweet, gently bred, blond softness. But perhaps a bit too slender; her cheeks were gaunt. And her dress and bonnet were of fine quality but thin from use, the ribbon frayed. "I called at your house first. Your manservant said that he had barely seen you in days. He sent me to another house, the home of Madame Étoile? Her parlor was so grand that I was afraid to sit down." She offered a takingly modest smile. "The lady of the house was not in, but her assistant said that I might find you here." She glanced about the office and seemed to notice Elle for the first time.

"Who is this, Masinter?" Charlie said. "Another poor female you're hoodwinking? Perhaps a bit of fluff on the side?"

The woman's eyes widened.

The captain stepped toward her. "M—"

"Madam, who are you to this man?" Charlie demanded.

"I—I am—" She gazed up at the captain mistily. "Captain Masinter has asked me to marry him. I am his betrothed."

~o0o~

There was a quality of nightmare to the next minutes that Elle could not overcome, no matter how she tried to remind herself that she had fully anticipated this, that she had even experienced it before, in this very room, and therefore should not be surprised that her insides were twisting in knots of sticky hot pain, and the blood all draining from her face and hands.

But she had not really experienced *this* before. She had not been in love with Josiah Junior, only infatuated with a lying scoundrel. Which, she supposed, was the case this time too.

He had taken the woman—*his betrothed*—out of the shop and was speaking with her now on the street. Through the window Elle could see his face, grave and sober, even the taut muscles in his jaw.

"I told you, Gabrielle," Charlie said as she turned from the window and went into the press room. "You mustn't trust—"

"Then whom can I trust, Charlie?" She looked him directly in the eye. "Shall I go through life imagining every member of the male sex a vain, rapacious egoist like your brother? Shall I dampen all my wishes for companionship and affection, and fear all attachments because some wretched man might someday hurt my feelings? Is that how you would prefer that I go along? Is it?"

"No," he said in an oddly strangled voice. "I don't want that for you at all."

The captain came into the doorway. "May I speak with you?" he said to her carefully, firmly, and despite all she felt her heart squeeze.

She nodded, passed him by, and left the shop. His betrothed was nowhere in sight. The carriage that he had purchased to celebrate bachelorhood was parked on the street. He gestured toward it.

She climbed up onto the seat without accepting his hand for assistance. A flat nausea was filling her. She could not look at him.

"You are betrothed," she said as he guided the team away from Brittle & Sons.

"Technically. Not actually."

"What does that mean?"

"I don't know."

"But you did ask for her hand?"

"Yes."

"You should not—you should not have . . . kissed me." And touched her and made her feel like she was flying.

"I shouldn't have. But not for the reason you believe." There was certainty in his tone. She wanted him to be confused and miserable, like she was.

"She is lovely," she said.

He did not reply; his lips were a line.

"Do you admire her?"

"Don't particularly know her."

"You do not *know* her?"

"Not really."

"But, the children—"

His gaze snapped to her, surprisingly hard. "*Not* mine." He looked forward again and his hands readjusted the reins. "Fond of them, though."

"Is it an arranged marriage?"

"No."

Elle folded and refolded her fingers in her lap. "She is obviously the daughter of a gentleman." Despite the wear in her clothing. "Does she have a fortune you want?" she said skeptically.

"No."

"She *is* very lovely."

"She's a fine looking woman."

The sick ache in her stomach finally sealed her lips.

"I owe you an explanation," he said. "But I can't give it, Elle. Not—That is, not now." His face was severe. "Matter of honor."

"*Honor?*"

"Not *my* honor. Mine's sailed away on an easterly, obviously."

"I think I hate you for not telling me before," she said.

"You should. But, by God, I wish you didn't. Of all the people in the world—"

"Of all the people in the world you would not wish to offend, I am at the top of the list," she said with intentional blandness. "I certainly believe that."

"Don't," he said shortly. "I don't deserve your forgiveness, but I haven't given you cause to believe I'm a heartless villain. I should have— Didn't expect—" He exhaled hard. "I didn't know."

"You did not know that I would throw myself at you yesterday? Well, you need not flagellate yourself, Captain. I am not a society belle whose maidenly modesty must be preserved at all costs until marriage. Nor am I a foolish girl, but a woman grown who has made mistakes in the past and learned from them. This time I knew what I was doing. And I enjoyed it. Not only yesterday, but this entire fantastical interlude. It is true that I wish we had succeeded in replacing the type. But it was never your responsibility to do so, and I am actually glad for having had this diversion from my troubles for a short while. So, really, you have nothing about which to feel guilty."

"Are you speaking sincerely?" he said tightly.

"Of course I am." But the dull pain in her chest gave lie to that. "Where are you taking me?"

"Home."

His home? He *wouldn't*.

"Suspect you'd like the company of your grandmother about now," he said.

She shut her eyes against a fresh surge of misery. How could a man so compassionate be a profligate flirt? It was not right. It was not fair. But life was never fair. She had known that long before she met Captain Anthony Masinter.

"Why did you come with me?" he said. "Just now."

"I wanted to be away from Charlie's accusations. And I was not yet prepared to tell him about the missing type."

"Let me help you, Elle."

"He will notice it soon enough. Perhaps he already has."

"Till you're certain of it, I'm your man. We'll work out something."

"No. This time there truly is no *we*, Captain. Your part in this is finished."

"Can't bear seeing your pretty eyes dulled. All because of what I've done."

"I cannot believe you lied to me!" she burst out. "I cannot believe I thought that you were a man of integrity."

"Blast it, I *am* a man of integrity, at least where you're concerned. I never lied to you, Elle."

"How can you insist on this when I now know the truth?"

"You do know the truth, the truth that I've lied to everybody for a decade." He halted the carriage before her building. "And you know all the other truths of any importance. You know that I find you clever and bold and beautiful and sweet and rich as butter, that you turn me inside out, that you're all I've thought about for days—you and that damn missing type," he growled.

"I do not wish to hear any more of this. I should not have gotten into this carriage."

He clapped a big, beautiful hand over his face. "Confound it!"

"Confound what?" She hated the note of desperation in her own voice.

"Confound honor and duty and everything I've held dear for twenty years! Confound it that I asked a woman I don't know to marry me because her husband was a friend and I'm to blame for his death. Confound it that they went and had three children, and now mother and children haven't a penny left or a relative in the country and she won't accept charity, but I can't leave 'em like that. And confound it that I knocked you over that night, because I wasn't too keen on the plan already, never intended to marry, perfectly happy as a bachelor for the rest of my days, still I knew I had to fix this, but now I dread it because I'd give everything I have to kiss you even one more time. That's confound what, Miss Gabrielle Flood."

"You are at fault for your friend's death?" she said thinly.

"My first lieutenant. John Park."

"Your—He was—*he* was her husband?"

"Aye."

"What happened to him?"

"I taught him how to game. No. Didn't teach him. Forced him. Said a man's not a man if he don't ease up and enjoy himself in a calm sea. He did it to please me. But he took to the card table too well. Got in over his head. Couldn't pay his debts."

"I don't understand. How did he die?"

He stared over the horses' ears.

"How?" she prodded.

"He put a pistol in his mouth."

"*Oh*, Anthony." She moved close and looked up into his face. "You mustn't blame yourself because a man could not control his gambling."

"I should have known."

She laid a hand on his arm and pressed her fingertips into his sleeve.

"You are not God. You cannot predict another's actions."

He looked down at her hand. "I can mend what I've broken."

She drew away. "Like you wish to mend my mistake, though it was not truly your fault. It was my misdeed. I must shoulder the blame. Alone."

"I won't allow it."

"I am not one of your crewmen, Captain. You cannot order me to obey you."

"By God, when you speak to me like that, I want to—"

"Make me swab the deck?" She offered him a little smile.

"Kiss you. I want to kiss you again more than I want to breathe." But he was not looking at her lips. He was looking into her eyes.

"You may not."

"I realize that."

He swept his hand over his face. "Blast it." Then he dismounted the carriage and came around it to her. He stood so tall and straight, as though he were on the deck of a ship. He offered his hand, but she climbed down without taking it. He remained by the carriage as she went to the door, then paused.

"Will you . . ." She mustn't do this. But she was not as strong as her grandmother believed, and she needed this. That she realized it only now made her heart ache even more fiercely. "Will you come inside and allow me to introduce you to my grandmother?"

All expression deserted his features.

"She has been hoping to meet you. She is very ill, and I think a visit would buoy her spirits. And you . . ."

He tilted his head forward, his eyes questioning.

"You smell good," she said. "And you sound—you *sound* so good. Your voice. Your tread. So confident and yet peaceful, as though all the world is well."

"My tread?"

A wobbly smile broke over her lips and Tony's chest constricted like a vise was tightening around his ribs. That she could smile now made him want to scoop her up in his arms and never let her go.

"You will understand, inside," she said. "Would you?"

He nodded.

When they entered the flat, he knew that as long as he lived he would never forget the sight of it. It was small, smaller than his quarters aboard the *Victory*, the furniture of modest quality and old, and the upholstery and drapes threadbare. Poverty blanketed the place like channel fog, but a quiet dignity fought against it in details throughout. On the minuscule table in the galley were carefully arranged a pressed linen laid neatly with plate, chipped porcelain cup and spoon, and the pieces of type they had taken from his uncle's house. Above the sofa hung an embroidered sampler of the sort he'd never been able to read as a child. And painted on the walls around a closed door, roses bloomed in spectacular profusion from vines that scrolled up the doorposts and over the lintel.

Dignity and beauty, despite all. Like her.

He wanted to return to Brittle & Sons and wring her employer's neck for paying her so little, to demand that the world give this woman what she deserved. He didn't have the right, of course, and she would hate him for it. More than she already did.

Rapping softly on the closed door, she slipped inside. After a moment, she opened it wide for him.

"Captain . . . welcome." Nearly swallowed in a rocking chair beneath thick blankets, the woman was gray-haired, her flesh spare, her eyes glimmering—and unseeing. Tony had known eyes like this woman's, and he knew immediately that Elle's grandmother was blind.

Nevertheless, he bowed.

"Madam," he said, "I am honored to make your acquaintance."

Elle's gaze turned to him full of gratitude. He did not deserve it. He deserved to be strapped to a mizzenmast and flogged.

They remained in the bedchamber for several minutes. Elle was affectionate with her grandmother, and solicitous, but not noxiously so. When her grandmother's lids drooped, he bade her good day and went into the other room.

Coming out shortly and closing the door, Elle offered him a quick smile.

"Thank you," she said.

"The printing type," he said. "You wanted her to feel it."

"At the governor's printing shop in Virginia, my grandfather worked as a pressman and my grandmother proof-corrected pages. Twenty years ago, she suffered a fever and was very ill. She lost her eyesight and with it her position at the shop. Then one day my grandfather borrowed five composing sticks filled with type, without telling his employer." Her eyes were alight.

"Presumably he was not bowled over by a scoundrel while carrying them home?"

"He taught Gram how to read the type with her fingertips. It was some time before she did it with perfect accuracy. But eventually they proved her skill to the chief printer and he hired her anew. I wanted to give her that pleasure, just once, before—" Her voice caught and she turned her face away.

"Did you paint the roses?"

She looked at the twining trellis. "My grandfather did. Roses were always her favorite scent, especially after she lost her sight. When he fell ill with the black cough and we moved to London from the countryside so that I could take the position at Brittle and Sons, she missed the roses in our little garden dreadfully. My wages were never sufficient to purchase real roses, and my grandfather was obliged to stop working. But before he died he painted them so that . . ."

"So that you would never forget."

Her eyes were clear. "Please drive me back to the shop now, Captain."

She did not speak to him on the short drive, but when he dismounted and came to her side of the curricle, she took his hand and allowed him to assist her down. Her fingers trembled against his palm.

"It is far past lunchtime," she said, pulling her hand away and tucking it in her skirt. "I am a bit shaky from that."

She was lying now, and he had caused this too. "I will see you inside."

"No, I—"

"I will see you inside."

Charles Brittle sat behind a desk in the front room.

"Are you well, Gabrielle?" he said with a frown at Tony.

"I am."

"Brittle, go into the other room and shut the door. I've a word to say to Miss Flood and I don't wish to do so on the street."

The printer's eyes flared. "Of all the—"

"Now. Or you will soon regret it."

Brittle looked to Elle, and she nodded. He went.

When the door closed, Elle turned astonished eyes up to him. "This is *his* shop."

"I am sorry for this muddle I've made. But sorry won't cut it, I know. I should have told you about John Park, his widow, from the start."

"You should have, but I understand why you did not. Whatever the case, it is now at an end and I will be glad to shake hands and wish you well, Captain."

He scowled. "I won't shake your damned hand— dashed—*damn it*."

"I certainly will not allow you to *kiss* me good-bye."

"You think I'd—?" He broke off and swung his gaze away. Then he looked her straight in the eyes with all the intensity of his Mediterranean stare. "Will you accept him?"

"Accept whom?"

"Your champion." His nostrils flared. "Charles Brittle."

"Accept him for what? Oh! Oh, no. You have mistaken it. Charlie and I are good friends. Were, that is, until today. But we are quite like brother and sister, you see. He accused you because he worries for me. Ever since Jo Junior—well—that is to say, Charlie only wishes to protect me."

"He wishes to do more than protect you, Elle."

She stepped back. "Now, you should leave. I must tell Charlie the truth about the type before he discovers it himself."

"If they are unforgiving, if they seek to punish you, you must send for me."

"I shan't need you. I can manage well on my own."

It seemed he would reply. Instead he went to the door, but paused there.

"Captain," she said before he could speak, "I do not want to see you again."

With a stiff bow he donned his hat and reached for the handle. The door opened wide and Jo Junior stepped into the shop.

"Damn that traffic, Charlie! Hattie complained of the heat the—Oh, I beg your pardon, sir!" His skin glowed, his hair was light with sun, his coat was the height of fashion, and he looked like gold-plated nickel beside a solid guinea. "How do you do?" He bowed and smiled ingratiatingly. Elle could see him already calculating the costliness of the captain's coat, the quality of his starched linen, the signet ring on his beautiful hand.

Jo's gaze flicked to her. "G'day, Gabby." Then he returned his sparkling smile to the captain. "Welcome to Brittle and Sons, sir. Allow me to introduce myself. I am Josiah Brittle, proprietor of—"

"Is this him?" The captain looked at her.

"Is this *he*," she whispered. "Yes."

He hit him, a quick, sudden swing of his bunched fist that barreled into Jo Junior's jaw and sent him staggering back into the doorframe with a shout.

"What in the—"

And the captain hit him in the nose.

This time Jo Junior went to the floor, tripping over the umbrella bin and hat stand and sprawling onto his behind with a clatter of furniture, groans, and crude oaths. Blood flowing from his nose and eyes wide, he cowered in the corner.

The captain loomed over him.

"If you ever again abuse this woman in any manner—" His voice was like gravel. "If you say one displeasing word to her or disturb a single hair on her head, I will return here and remove your limbs from your torso, one limb at a time. Understood?"

Mouth agape, Jo Junior nodded.

Calmly picking up his hat from where it had fallen to the floor, the captain set it on his shiny locks, bowed to her, and departed, taking her laughter and her heart with him.

Chapter Twelve

When Mr. Brittle Senior returned from Bristol two days later, Elle stood beside Charlie and retold the tale of the missing type.

"A body's bound to make a mistake in life now and again," Mr. Brittle said, tucking his thumbs into his waistcoat that was stretched from quite a lot of good life. That his good life was paid for by her hard labor and Lady Justice's demands for equality struck Elle now as remarkably hypocritical. But he was studying her thoughtfully, considering mercy, and she needed this position.

"I could withhold your wages until the cost of the missing type is recouped," he said.

"Of course." She would throw herself upon the charity of Mr. Curtis. She would take in sewing work. She would not buy milk or eggs, only enough for her grandmother until...

"But trust is essential in business, Miss Flood," he said. "And with this little escapade you've broken my trust."

"Mr. Brittle, I understand that broken trust is difficult to mend." She understood it intimately. "But—"

"Then you'll understand why I have to let you go."

The numbness settled in instantly. No need to flare into panic or distress, after all. She knew this road well.

"Very well," she said. She cast a final glance through the press room doorway, to the desk and work that had been her life for eight years, until a captain in the Royal Navy who could barely read two words on a page came along. Lady Justice's latest pamphlet was still in the frame and the pressmen were running the pages, one sheet after another with well-practiced fluidity, printing the pamphlets that would be sold on street corners throughout London tomorrow. Pamphlets that would net Brittle & Sons many hundreds of pounds.

Anger rose in her, swift and burning. Taking up her bonnet, she went to the door.

"Father, please," Charlie said behind her. "You cannot—"

"No, Charlie," she said. "Do not beg on my behalf. It is beneath you. And it is beneath me. Good-bye now." She left the shop, and walked home. When she passed the grate in the cobbles in the alley, the place where she had lost much more than a few pieces of metal, she did not even look down.

~o0o~

"You did *what?*" The Earl of Bedwyr was gaping.

"Heard me the first time," Tony growled.

"I heard you, but I still cannot fathom it."

"Would've done the same yourself."

"I would most certainly not have asked a woman to marry me for those reasons, you chivalrous numbskull. You are the only fool here with more honor than sense." The earl wagged his head. "Idiot."

"So glad I stopped by, Charles. Can't tell you how much this is helping."

"Imbecile."

For a moment the only sound in the room was the ticking of a clock on the mantel.

"And you say she refused you at first, but then changed her mind?"

"Said she thought it over more carefully."

"How inconveniently fickle of her. Why didn't you simply tell her that she had lost her chance?"

"Because I ain't as much of a scoundrel as you, I guess."

Scoundrel.

Tony sank his face into his hands, but Elle's soft, saucy eyes were before him every time he closed his, and he wanted a gangplank and a shark-infested sea to throw himself into.

No. He wanted *her*. He wanted her so much he could taste her—feel her in his hands—smell her hair and skin.

"What will you do?" Cam said. "Marry the widow and her multiple children?"

"Poor thing's got no one. No family. No money. I can't leave her and the little ones to the streets."

"Mm," his friend agreed grimly. "Or the workhouse."

Yet if Brittle threw off Elle, she would be in the same boat.

No. That wasn't so. Gabrielle Flood had too much spirit, too much good sense, too much intelligence and gumption and daring and willful verve to ever surrender. For God's sake, she had masqueraded as a Hungarian princess at a society ball. Also, she didn't have three little ones to feed, clothe, and house. And hundred to one, some man—*some man better than him*—would come along, give her his name, set her up in a fine cottage, provide her with children of her own, and she would make him the happiest fellow on land or sea.

Tony stared at the palms of his hands. Hers were always stained with ink: the fingertips, knuckles, even the palms sometimes. He suspected she didn't even realize it. Or care. She had a mind and heart bent to a single devotion.

If she were his, he'd buy her a printing house.

He wanted to do it now. He would instruct his solicitor to start looking for a building, and a printing press for sale. He ached to give her what she deserved.

It couldn't be. If Jane Park had plenty of reasons to reject a gift from a man who wasn't her husband, Elle had even better reasons. And he would not open her to the potential shame of others misconstruing it.

Perhaps someday—an anonymous gift of a printing press—long after she'd forgotten all about him and would not guess where it came from...

The notion of that future without her was so bleak, he groaned.

"It seems to me that you are going about this all wrong, Anthony," his friend said, echoing the words Elle had recited to him days ago from Peregrine's letter to Lady Justice. Bedwyr was a writer too, of course. He knew how to turn a pretty phrase. She wanted that. She admired eloquence; she'd nearly fallen over when she'd met Bedwyr.

Even if he were free of his responsibility to the widow, Elle would never accept him.

"That so?" he snarled. "How d'you suppose I should go about it, then?"

The earl's eyes widened. "Do you know," he said, "I have never—not once, not when Westfall was bleeding into the sand and you were beside yourself with grief, not when your damn brother tried to contest your great-aunt's will and steal Maitland Manor away from you, not even when Seraphina told you the truth about her marriage—I have never seen you so distraught. I never even imagined it was in your nature to be so."

"It ain't." *Isn't.* He dragged air into his lungs, but they would not fill.

Cam sat forward. "Anthony, you broke through French blockades. And for your entire life you have destroyed even greater obstacles than that. You must devise a solution to this problem that does not require you to marry the widow, one that will satisfy both your honor and Mrs. Park's future. The unlucky past must not command you now."

The unlucky past.

Unlucky.

The past...

The past.

A memory came to him then in a flash, like Saint Elmo's Light in a squall: *Standing beside John Park on the quarterdeck, looking out across a placid sea, John chuckling, telling the story of how he had met his wife through a midshipman he'd met in port. "The fellow shipped out the day he'd planned to propose to her. He said he and Jane were childhood sweethearts, and he sent me to tell her to wait for him. She couldn't, of course. She hadn't a shilling, her parents had died, and she had no friends in port. Only him." John grinned. "His delay was my win. He had waited too long, unlucky bastard."*

Tony leaped from his chair and flew out of the room.

"Uncle Anthony!" Margaret called as he descended the stairs three at a time. "Why are you running?"

"Nurse says we mustn't run in the house, Captain," Letty said.

Scooping them from the bannister where they were hanging like monkeys, he hauled them up in his arms and kissed the top of each little head. They giggled and he set them down, and grabbed his hat from the footman. Donning it at a scoundrelly angle, he bowed to the mites.

"Ladies, I'm off to Newcastle."

"Bring presents for us!" Margaret squealed.

"Of course." But he intended to bring much more than presents. He would bring a miracle.

~o0o~

Elle did not tell her grandmother about losing her position at the shop, or anything about the captain. Instead she gathered up several of the smallest pieces of the bishop's type from the kitchen table, laid them upon her grandmother's palm, and curled her fingers around them. A ghost of a smile fluttered over the pale lips.

"Dear . . . girl."

Elle tucked the coverlet around Gram's frail body, kissed her on the brow, and whispered her love.

"I like him." The words came so softly from her grandmother's mouth, Elle barely heard them.

"I do too." Despite herself. "Good night, darling." Elle left her grandmother to sleep, passing beneath the painted trellis of roses that she had not really seen in years, not until he reminded her of them, and went to bed.

The following morning when she tried to rouse her grandmother to take breakfast, Gram would not wake.

The morning after that was the same.

Two mornings later, she was gone.

~o0o~

The funeral was modest, held in a sunny corner of the foundling home's cemetery. Before falling ill, Elle's grandmother had often visited the children to tell them stories. She had been beloved in their little community, Mr. and Mrs. Curtis said, but Elle suspected they did this to spare her the expense of a burial elsewhere.

As she stood beside the hole in the ground, with dry eyes she watched the gravedigger pile dirt onto the plain wooden box and wondered how Captain Masinter had felt watching his lieutenant buried. She knew he must have watched; his sense of responsibility for others was acute.

Minnie and Esme were waiting for her at the gate.

"Come have a cuppa, Elle," Minnie said. "I will treat for biscuits."

"Thank you. But I must look about for a new position today."

"Elle, no." Esme said. "Not today."

But biscuits today would not transform into dinner tomorrow, or rent at the end of the month.

"Madame Couture will hire you until you can find another post," Minnie said. "All the society ladies will soon return to town. She will need extra seamstresses."

"Thank you, dear friends." Elle squeezed their hands. "But I have a plan." She had the direction of an employment agency across town and a burning need to be as far from Brittle & Sons, Printers, as possible. Lady Justice's latest pamphlet was on every street corner, but Elle hadn't even the pennies to purchase a copy. It was foolish to want the final broadsheet. But it was the last of the correspondence between the pamphleteer and her nemesis that Elle had shared with Gram. And because of it she had met a ship captain who opened up her heart again.

That heart beat now shallowly. Emptily. It did not even ache. Instead, she was numb. She would feel again someday, perhaps. For now she must find work.

When she bade her friends goodbye, however, she did not walk in the direction of the employment agency. She walked home. She needed to sit in the rocking chair by her grandmother's bed. And she needed to see the roses that her grandfather had painted on the walls, to feel the power of love and devotion that even in misfortune had never died.

The grocer's boy perched on the building's stoop. Leaping up and tearing off his cap, he mumbled, "I'm that sorry, miss."

"Thank you, Sprout. She always appreciated your help."

"She, miss?"

"My grandmother."

He cocked his head curiously.

"I have just come from her funeral."

His eyes popped wide. "Gor blimey, miss. I didn't know!" Then his nose screwed up. "S'pose the cap'n didn't either."

Elle's numb heart tripped. "The captain?"

Guilt washed over the boy's face. "I'm plum sorry for showin' him where the key's hidden."

Now her heart sped. "He asked you for the key to my flat?"

His head bobbed. "I tried not to tell him, miss. Honest! But he said if I didn't, he'd send the impressment crew over to nab me right up."

She imagined the gleam in the captain's eyes when he had made the empty threat, and she pinned her lips adamantly together. She did not want to smile now. She did not want to know his outrageous humor. She did not want to know *him*.

"After I showed him, I ran outta there quick, case he changed his mind and sent 'em anyway. Then I got to feelin' poorly about doin' you wrong. I'd to say how sorry I am for it, miss. Don't know what the cap'n wanted it for anyhow. Key's still under the mat." He shrugged.

"Then I guess we should investigate."

Sprout followed her up the stairs, her heart beating quicker with each step. When she reached the landing, she sensed something different. *A scent.* Bending to the mat, she took up the key and the scent positively overwhelmed. With shaky fingers she opened the door.

Roses.

Everywhere.

On tables. On the floor. In corners. Spilling out of vases and festooning chairs, on every surface pink and yellow and red and white blooms rampant with color. The most spectacular arrangements were clustered about her grandmother's bed, their glorious fragrance filling the air.

Elle's throat closed. Her eyes welled.

Finally, she wept.

~o0o~

Tony glowered at the page he'd been staring at for half an hour without making headway. It was like sailing against a damn trade wind, trying to make sense of the papers the land steward at Maitland Manor had sent. But he'd little knowledge of houses and fields, and he had to muddle through this quick primer. Couldn't ask a woman to share his estate till he knew it himself. But he was impatient to be done with it. The sooner he could get down on his knee before that woman again—this time without shoes in hand—the better.

The door of his sitting room swung open.

"Disturb me, Cob," he growled, "and I'll have you strung up from the crow's—"

But it was not Cob who stood there.

"You should not have done it." Her face was blotched, and streaked with tears, her hair disarranged, and her hands twisting a kerchief she obviously wasn't bothering to use because her nose was a bright soggy mess.

She looked like heaven.

"Why did you do it?" she demanded.

"She didn't like them?" He stood up and moved to her. "Blast it. I'm sorry, Elle. I wanted to—"

She threw herself upon his chest, pressed her face into his waistcoat, and a great sob shook her. He cupped his hands around her shoulders, wanting to grab her up entirely, to hold her. He'd needed her in his arms again like he needed air, but this was not precisely what he'd had in mind.

"Elle?" he said quietly.

"She is gone." Another sob convulsed her body. "She is gone."

"*Gone?*"

"In the night," she said muffled against his coat. "I buried her this morning."

"My God." He wrapped his arms tight around her.

She wept and he ached for her. He longed to say something comforting or profound. He stroked her hair, held her close, and felt her sobs in his body.

"You made her proud," he finally whispered. "I saw it, heard it in her voice. So proud."

She sobbed harder.

Blast it. He truly was an idiot with words.

Eventually the sobs subsided. With an enormous sniff, she lifted her sodden face. Stroking his thumb across her cheek, he wiped away tears.

"I'm sorry, Elle."

She blinked, scattering teardrops from her lashes. And abruptly the glimmer in her eyes changed. Then her gaze dropped to his lips.

Every muscle in his body went instantly on alert. *Every* muscle. He was the greatest scoundrel alive.

She pulled away, her damp gaze now slightly fevered and skittering up and down him, lighting him on fire.

"I should not have come here," she said.

"I'm glad you did." His voice sounded far too rough.

She stared at him, lips parted, her perfect breasts rising and falling on sharp breaths. He wanted her against him again. Not weeping, though. Sighing and moaning would do.

He locked himself in place. This was not the time, not with her grief so fresh. He could wait. He could wait forever if in the end she would be his.

"Elle, I—"

"Are you betrothed yet? *Actually* betrothed, not only technically? Or—" Her throat constricted. "Married?"

"*No.*" He swallowed hard. "I couldn't." Not as long as this woman walked the earth. "No."

"You . . . couldn't?"

"Of course not."

She flattened a palm to his ribs and pushed him back against the wall.

She climbed up him. Mouth claiming his, she clung to his shoulders and he scooped his hands around her soft behind and hitched her thighs up about his hips, and they kissed like that, ravenously, fantastically. Her mouth consuming his was hot and tasted of lust and the remnants of tears, and her hands were all over him, in his hair, around his jaw, under his coat, then beneath his shirt, and *he had to have her.* Now. The devil take grief and gentlemanly restraint and waiting for vows or anything else to be said. She was his and she always would be.

He carried her to his bed.

First her long sable locks came down, cascading over the white linen like silk, as he had dreamed. Her bodice followed, unfastened and then tugged until her breasts were bared entirely.

Her eyes were spectacularly wide, her cheeks and throat flushed, and the perfect, pink peaks of her breasts tight with arousal. Nothing would come to his tongue, no words, not even sound. Wrapping his hands around her waist, he bent his head and rested his brow between her breasts, and breathed her in.

Her fingers threaded into his hair.

"Won't you kiss me?" Her voice trembled.

"Everywhere you wish."

"For what are you waiting?"

"Trouble with banquets, a man don't always know where to begin."

Laughter tumbled from her. "A man *does n—*"

He captured her lips with his. Then he took her breasts in his hands, passed his thumbs across the peaks, and felt her gasp into his mouth. He bent his head and with his tongue tasted one beautiful nipple.

Within a minute she was dragging at his coat with her

eager hands, then his waistcoat, then his shirt, and groaning. When she arched her hips against his, he slipped his hand down her belly and between her legs and held her. The flavor of her skin was in his mouth, the texture of her beauty, her desire on his tongue, and he did not give her what she was urging him to give her swiftly.

This was his banquet. He would not be rushed.

Her body was strung like a leeward jib sheet, taut and straining. She whispered his name, then again more urgently. Her fingers scored paths along his arms, over his shoulders, into his hair again. He scraped his teeth over her nipple and she whimpered.

Now she was ready.

With the shift of his fingers over her skirts, he caressed her womanhood. She cried out. Thrusting her hips, convulsing against his caresses, she cried and cried again, sounds of desperation and ecstasy at once.

When her gasps subsided and her eyes opened, hazy and sated, she looked up at him. In all of his years sailing the seas, in every exotic land, upon every familiar shore, atop every magnificent swell and beneath every starlit night, her smile was the most beautiful thing he had ever seen.

He nearly took her then, immediately, half-dressed, wholly ready. He didn't. She deserved more. She deserved everything. So instead he cupped his hands around her perfect breasts, lowered his mouth to the neglected nipple, and said, "Second dish."

~o0o~

He undressed her one garment at a time. Between garment removals he made her wild with need. And he made her laugh. She had never imagined that there could be laughter in making love. But this was her scoundrel, so of course there was.

With kisses everywhere she wished—as he had promised—he brought to the surface all the longing and pleasure buried within her. Then, with kisses in places she had not even known *could* be kissed, he sent the pleasure deeper than she had known pleasure could go. It was all very new, delectably shocking, intensely delicious, and wonderful.

Just as wonderfully, he encouraged her to touch him, to undress him, caress him, and kiss him, also wherever she wished. By the time she was finally fully undressed, naked beneath him, and once again aching with need, she knew the contours of the muscles and sinews in his arms and chest and legs, the powerful beauty of his bared shoulders, and the thorough delirium of his skin against hers.

"Sweet Elle," he said against her throat. "I am well-seduced, entirely at your mercy, ravished beyond ravishment."

She laughed.

"Say you will have me now, Elle, or I'll perish at once."

Circling her hands around his arms, she smiled. "I will have you now, Captain."

He took her mouth beneath his and kissed her beautifully, deeply. Then she had him.

She did not know what to expect. Her memory of intimacy was a fog of pain and frustration.

This was *entirely* different.

"Good God, Elle," he said, his lips brushing her lips, his chest moving hard against hers as he grew still within her, a great big hot presence that was stretching her nearly beyond endurance. "It feels good to be inside you."

"You used a subject pronoun." She spread her palms over his shoulders. "You said *it.*"

"Overcome. Won't happen again." His hand found her breast. She moaned, his lips claimed hers, and she forgot all about discomfort and doubt and grammar.

"Now?" he said.

"Yes," she whispered, and there only languid, throbbing heat. And hunger.

His hand came between them. And then, with the caress of his fingers, he made her writhe. Pressing up to him, desperately hungry, she begged with her body.

Finally he moved in her, slowly at first, forcing moans of

need from her. Upon a firm, quick stroke of his fingertip he thrust deep. Then again. Then again until she was seeking him, needing more, needing everything. His hands grasped her wrists and he met her again and again, faster, harder, until she was begging for release, and then crying out when it came. His muscles hardened like rock and he spoke her name, powerfully, then again as he grew still.

Their bodies hot and slick, their breathing ragged, he tenderly brushed damp silk from her cheeks. Then he wrapped his arms around her and buried his face against her neck.

For the first time since they had met in an alleyway at dusk, they said nothing for quite some time. Twining her arms around his waist and tucking her head beneath his chin, she wept a little more, then fell asleep smiling.

~o0o~

Having traveled hundreds of miles yet rested little over the previous five days, Tony was unsurprised to discover that he had slept past dusk. The bedchamber door was ajar and a lamp glowed on the stairwell landing. In the dim light he saw no woman tangled in the bedclothes beside him.

He tugged his breeches on. None of the feminine garments he had removed from her were strewn about the room. But she must be nearby.

He found evidence of her in his sitting room. The little print mistress herself was not, however, present. In the center of his desk littered with papers was a handwritten note. With a peculiar sensation scraping the back of his throat, he took up the page of closely penned words and read.

When he came to the end of it, he lowered himself into a chair, drew a long, shaking breath, and read it again.

Then he read it again.

Folding it carefully, he went into his bedchamber to dress.

Chapter Thirteen

Elle was not a martyr by nature, only vastly unlucky, cursed by Fate, and scorned by heaven. Simply because she had suffered a lot of misery in life did not mean she actually *liked* it.

This present misery, however, took the prize. She loved two people and they were both gone, one by death, the other by her own effort.

Still, she did not weep. She had done plenty of that three days earlier in her flat, in a hackney cab, in his arms, then in his bed. And it seemed, after all, that she was not really the sort of person to weep from sorrow, only in joy.

He did not call on her, and for that she applauded her newfound talent for writing utter falsehoods: that she had given it quite a lot of thought and, while she liked him, she did not like him quite enough to continue with him; that she had decided to move to America where her grandparents had known Important People who could make her a success in the printing business; and finally that if he sought her out again she would write to the Admiralty and tell them what she knew. Vile to write, the lies had obviously satisfied her purpose. Now he must dislike her excessively, which suited her plan no matter how wretched she felt.

Returning from halfway across town after a third endless day waiting in the employment agency to be interviewed—without success—she dragged her aching feet and heart up to her flat. The roses were in full, magnificent bloom, the whole place awash in glorious perfume. She had already given away so many to her neighbors they were beginning to think her a florist. Perhaps that could be her next post. She would look for signs in shop windows that read: BROKEN-HEARTED FLOWER

Girls, Apply Within.

She went into her kitchen to make tea, and there were Minnie, Adela, Esme and Charlie, all in the tiny room.

"Good heavens, how are you here?"

"We walked over, of course," Adela said.

"Sprout told us where you hide the key," Esme said.

"I must find another hiding spot," Elle mumbled. But she needn't. Nobody would be visiting her grandmother here again. She was alone. It was her well-trodden path and inevitable, after all.

She had these caring friends, it was true; and for them she was deeply grateful.

"Elle," Minnie said disapprovingly. "You have made a terrible blunder."

Perhaps not so grateful. They could not possibly know what she had done, though. No one could. Not even the captain.

It had been wrong to open the seal and read the letter from Jane Park that she found buried under documents on his desk—by far the worst thing she had ever done. But such was her giddy post-love glow that she had assumed she would eventually be reading her lover's correspondence aloud to him anyway.

She could not regret it, nor taking the letter home to burn. He needn't ever know the contents of it: that in her husband's personal effects Jane had discovered the captain's secret, and that, starving and desperate and fearing for her children, she had sunk into such despair that she must now offer him only two choices. She would either write to the Admiralty detailing how her husband had gone beyond his regular duties in serving the captain of the *Victory*, and demand that they pay her a second, larger pension to make it right. Or Captain Masinter could stand by his offer to marry her. In the letter Jane had apologized to him—again and again in sweetly pious prose—but she said she had no other choice. Elle felt for the poor widow and her tiny children, and she suspected that under the circumstances she herself might do the same. Of course, she might simply ask him for a loan until she recouped her losses.

Or not.

One thing she had learned from adoring Jo Junior for years was that people did not always do what was in their own best interests.

On the other hand, it was definitely in Jane Park's interests to marry a wealthy aristocrat. Under the circumstances, blackmail was understandable. Even more important than the blackmail, however, was that Elle knew the captain's sense of responsibility and honor would not allow him happiness if Mrs. Park and her children suffered. Elle could not have borne that. Above all she wanted his happiness.

"What mistake?" she said to Minnie.

Charlie stepped forward. "You should not have given up so easily." He proffered a letter. It was the stationery upon which Lady Justice sent messages to Brittle & Sons, with the name Gabrielle Flood above the address. "It arrived this morning."

"What—What is it?" she said weakly.

"Read it," Esme said.

"It has already been opened." Cosmic retribution, no doubt.

"My brother's doing, of course," Charlie said. "I beg your pardon for that." He was watching her thoughtfully, and for the first time she saw in his eyes that which for years she had denied: affection beyond anything she could return. She had never wanted to see it because she did not wish to then be obliged to reject it, and lose his friendship. Since her grandfather's death, Charlie had been the only man she trusted other than Mr. Curtis. Now she knew what it was to love, to truly love, and she hurt for him.

"Read it, Gabrielle," he said.

The hand was neat and firm: the hand of her hero, Lady Justice.

Dear Miss Flood,
Yesterday I received a letter from a gentleman claiming that,

although he has no right to write to me on your behalf, he doubted you would do so yourself. He begged me to rectify the wrong that he and your employer did to you in the matter of fifty-three pieces of missing printer's type. Given the narrative he offered, I agree: you should not be punished for this unfortunate mishap. Moreover, I am indebted to you for years of service to me, and therefore to all of Britain. My message is more effective because of your labors.

I have informed Mr. Brittle that if he does not reinstate you in your position, immediately raise your wages by thirty percent, and subsequently five percent per annum, I will find another publisher.

Your gentleman admirer also told me of your wish to collect within a single volume a selection of my work and letters of that pompous narcissist who continues to write to me despite my disdain of everything for which he stands. I think it a travesty to reprint the utterings of that elitist cretin, but if it will help spread the message of Justice into more parlors throughout Britain, I will encourage Mr. Brittle to make it so.

One more detail of this matter moves me now to speak to you as a friend. As all know, I often publish letters that I receive from members of the aristocracy, especially if they reveal injustices. In his letter to me your admirer exposed his heart as well as a vulnerability that, given his identity, could ruin him if made public, or at the very least open him to great censure. He showed no concern over this, only honesty in his wishes for your wellbeing.

I have destroyed his letter. I will not print it, for I believe that selflessness should be rewarded. Don't you agree?

In sincere gratitude for your labor,
Lady Justice

Elle lifted to her friends eyes filled with tears.

"Will you return to Brittle and Sons, Gabrielle?" Charlie said.

"Yes." It was a bittersweet victory. She had her work. She would never have her captain. God, it seemed, was merciful. But Fate was a vindictive tease.

~o0o~

Elle returned to the shop the following morning. Jo Junior, who still sported a bruised nose, glowered at her. But he offered her his own desk at which to work.

She declined. She liked her spot in the corner of the printing room, with its scent of ink and the big solid comfort of the press and its companion tray full of type.

Charlie brought her a cup of tea.

"What a nice surprise," she said. He had never before brought her anything. That Captain Masinter had brought her a glass of ale—*and something extra*—within minutes of meeting her tweaked her heart with fresh aching.

"Welcome back, Gabrielle," Charlie said only, and left her to the pile of paper that had accumulated in her brief absence.

Mr. Brittle Senior stopped by the shop midmorning, spoke to her cheerfully about the usual sorts of things, and never once mentioned what had passed. The missing type was forgotten. Lady Justice had prevailed. Rather, Mr. Brittle's greed. But such was the nature of business, she supposed.

At lunchtime the clerk and the pressmen went off to the King's Barrel, and Charlie and Jo Junior departed for a meeting across town. The shop was empty and Elle sat with her pen and a page of the latest edition of *Falconer's Dictionary of the Marine* and went through every line with her usual thoroughness, despite the lump in her throat. That she must work now on a nautical dictionary was simply more cosmic retribution. But at least she was learning interesting details about the life he had led for years.

The shop door jingled and Elle slid off her stool and went into the front room.

Jane Park stood there in all her sweet blond loveliness. She wore a yellow gown and a smart new pelisse and bonnet with shiny ribbons, and she carried a reticule made of silk.

Elle considered the disadvantages of becoming ill all over her employer's floor.

"Good—" she forced over the grotesquely huge prickly ache in her throat. "Good day."

Jane's pale eyes blinked like a little startled woodland

creature's. There was no intelligence in those eyes, nothing interesting, nothing to make a naval captain laugh or scowl. The nausea in Elle's stomach redoubled. She had thrown him into the arms of this woman and she wasn't at all certain that it had not been an incredibly foolish mistake made at a moment when her emotions were far too agitated with grief and joy and so much love and probably exhaustion.

"You were here the other day when I came to find Captain Masinter, weren't you?" the pale loveliness said.

"Yes. I—" She cleared her throat. "I work here. Everyone else has gone for lunch."

"You have such a kind smile, like the captain's," Jane Park said sweetly. "You seem like a person who would help a woman in need."

Tragically true. "How may I assist you?"

"My husband recently perished, leaving me and our children all alone in the world. Since then, the captain has been so generous. I want to give him something special, a gift, now that the wedding is going forward."

"A—" *Remember to breathe.* "A gift?"

"Oh, yes. A very special gift that he will cherish. I have an idea for it, but I don't know if it is a good idea. May I have your opinion on it?"

Apparently Jane understood the gurgling noise that came from Elle's mouth as assent.

"You see," Jane continued, "Captain Masinter and my late husband were wonderfully fond, and they spent hours pouring over ship's logbooks together. I found several pages from one of those books in my late husband's belongings. I thought I might have a page framed for display, for the captain, to show him my eternal gratitude for what he has done for me and my children."

Elle nearly sobbed.

"But I don't know a thing about pages or paper or frames." Jane offered a bewildered smile. "After he insulted me the other day, Mr. Charles Brittle apologized with such gentlemanly grace that I decided to come here and ask his advice. But I would be grateful for your thoughts instead. You must be very clever with books and paper."

"A little." *Although vastly un-clever with matters of the heart.*

"Also," Jane added, a twinkle in her eyes, "my fiancé is waiting outside in the carriage with my children. I should not make them wait long."

Elle's stomach turned over.

"Your idea is fine," she said slowly. "But I believe ship's logbooks are meant to be confidential rather than displayed on the wall."

"Oh. Yes. I suppose that is true." A haunted shadow crossed Jane's face. *Guilt.* Elle could read it in the woman's guileless eyes like she could read a page: Jane was remembering her blackmail scheme and hating herself for it.

Elle did not know how much more wringing a human heart could endure. And the notion that if she turned her head and looked out the window, she would see him, made every part of her weak with longing. She must end this immediately.

"I recommend not pursuing this idea," she said. "Instead"—she snatched up pen and paper—"there is a wonderful map shop at this address. It so happens that the proprietor sells beautiful nautical charts suitable for hanging on the wall. I am certain you will find one that is ideal for the captain." She proffered the paper.

"What a perfect idea!" The twinkle had returned to Jane's eyes. "Thank you, Miss—"

"That is not important, of course." Swiftly she ushered Jane to the door. "What matters is that he is happy. Now, good day to—" Her gaze caught on the wheel of the fine carriage parked before the shop, then swept along its side, then over the three adorable little towheads in the back, then up to the box.

It was not his carriage. It was not his team of matched grays. And the man standing beside it and gazing with besotted eyes at Jane Park was not *her captain.*

Jane said, "There is my fiancé! Do you see how grateful I am to the captain? He has made possible for me such happiness." Beaming into the man's face, she allowed him to hand her up into the carriage.

For a paralyzed moment Elle watched it move down Gracechurch Street. Then she dragged shut the door to Brittle & Sons, locked it, and hailed a hackney.

~o0o~

Captain Masinter was not at home. No one was. Mr. Cob did not answer her knock on the front door, and when she went around to the rear entrance no one answered there either. Even the stable boy was not in sight. Neither were the captain's big horse nor his new carriage and pair.

She found another hackney cab and went to Seraphina's house. Penelope told her that Madame Étoile had gone to call on Lady Bedwyr to make alterations on a gown, and she gave her the address.

But when Elle arrived at the elegant home of Lord and Lady Bedwyr, she did not find the modiste fitting anybody for a gown. Instead, in a spectacularly luxurious drawing room Seraphina was sitting with the earl and countess around a tea table, speaking closely and quietly.

The footman announced her and the earl rose languidly to his feet and bowed. But his dark eyes were hard. The ladies did not smile or even nod in greeting. None of them said a thing.

"Good—Good day," Elle stuttered.

They continued to stare without pleasure.

"I—I wonder if you might tell me—if, that is, you know where Captain Masinter could be. At the present moment," she added idiotically, twisting her fingers in the ribbon of her pelisse and entirely unable to cease doing so.

Finally Seraphina stood up.

"He is at the docks," she said. "His ship departs in five days."

"His ship? Five—Five *days?*"

"Yes, Miss Flood," the earl said. "Our friend has decided that a bachelor's life at sea is much more to his liking than the alternative. Now I wonder how he came to that decision? Hm?"

"No!" she blurted. "He mustn't go. Why is he *going*?"

"Well, what else did you expect my brother to do after you broke his heart?" Seraphina said. "He is a sailor."

"But—but—"

"But what?" the earl said grimly.

"He is the son of a *baronet*," Elle exclaimed. "He is a victorious naval captain. His closest friends are earls and princesses, for goodness' sake."

They stared at her.

Her composure broke. "Why doesn't anyone seem to have noticed that I am not his social equal?"

"I daresay because he has not," the earl said.

"Miss Flood," the countess said, "We have just now been discussing how we could convince Anthony not to depart like this. Yet we are stymied. Have you, perhaps, any idea that might meet with success?"

"I think I have."

Abruptly, all three of them looked a lot less hateful and a lot more hopeful.

Within minutes Elle was tucked into the corner of the earl and countess's carriage and flying across town.

Having adamantly avoided sailors until very recently, Elle had never been to the London docks. Stepping out of the carriage, she was overwhelmed. There was industry everywhere, from the quays busy with people going and coming, and carts laden with goods and pulled by massive horses, to the dozens of little boats moving here and there in the water, and to the decks of massive ships parked alongside the docks.

She allowed her gaze to follow the nearest ship's central mast up its noble length to the top that poked into the summer blue sky, and a wonderful calm blanketed her. This was his world, the world that had embraced him when others had rejected him, the world that had seen in a boy—a boy who could barely speak, read, or write—a hero.

It was also, however, a vast world and she hadn't any idea where to start looking for him. The coachman helped. Mentioning the captain by name, he gained them entrance onto the closest wharf. Another man that looked vaguely official pointed them toward a ship flanking a dock.

She found him there.

He stood on the highest deck of the massive vessel, so confident and *captain-like* that her heart gave itself one last violent squeeze, decided it was through with wringing forever, and abruptly ceased functioning. She mounted the gangplank and walked on wobbly knees to the deck. Covered with crates and barrels and ropes and sailors working diligently, the wooden planks seemed to stretch a mile to the stairs that led up to the deck upon which she had glimpsed him.

Then he was there, at the top of those steps, looking at her.

With her nonfunctioning heart in her throat, she went forward. He descended the steps and met her partway.

As though by magic all the sailors seemed to vanish.

"How did you do that?" burbled from her lips.

His beautifully intense eyes frowned. "What?"

"Clear the deck. Do they always part for you when you walk through, like the Red Sea for Moses?"

"Cob saw you board. I suspect he thought I'd prefer it." He did not laugh as she had hoped he would, or even smile. She could not fool herself that this was his captain's demeanor. She knew it was her presence here.

Without speaking he moved to the railing where a rope was dangling from a mast far above. Taking it into the big strong hands that she loved, he affixed it to a device attached to the rail and pulled.

"Why are you here?" he said over his shoulder.

"Where are you going?"

He paused in his task, but his hand remained on the rope, his coat strained across his shoulders. "Why do you want to know?"

"Well." Nerves in a tangle, she moved toward him. "I was

wondering if you are heading to Hungary, if I could perhaps come along and act as your translator."

He twined the rope about a metal bracket. "Quit with the teasing."

"All right. But does that mean I must quit with you too?"

"Can't quit what you never started, can you?"

"What if I want to start?" she said, then cleared her throat and said clearly. "With you."

Abruptly he turned to her.

"With *me*?" His eyes were stormy. "You threatened me. *Me*."

"It was wrong. *I* was wrong. I did not mean any of it. I thought—"

"You thought what? You thought that you could make love to a man like you care about him and then leave him with callous threats dashed across a scrap of paper, which, by the by, it took him an agonizing quarter of an hour to read, and he still wasn't certain he'd understood it correctly because frankly he was shocked, and astonished, so just to be certain he got it right he took it to his *sister* to confirm, which was its own unique kind of mortification. Is that what you thought?"

She couldn't speak. She nodded.

"Do you know what, Gabrielle Flood? *You* are a scoundrel."

"I *am* a scoundrel. I asked you to make love to me even though I knew there would be nothing between us afterward. I wanted to be with you so much that I didn't care it was wrong."

He walked right up to her and looked down into her face. "I am not Josiah Brittle Junior. That you can believe for even an instant that I made love to you with dishonorable intentions—"

"I thought you would never forgive yourself if you did not offer for Mrs. Park. You want the best for everybody, even when you cannot possibly be responsible for everybody. Still, you try to make it better. I could not bear to be the cause of you never making peace with your lieutenant's death."

"You were wrong," he said. "I made my peace with it."

"You did? How?"

"I hounded down her long-lost love."

"Her long-lost—*Oh*." She had seen him on Gracechurch Street: Jane's fiancé in the carriage with the children.

"Got lucky, admittedly. Fellow'd just returned from the East Indies. But I wouldn't have stopped searching till I'd found somebody to take her in and keep her safe so she wouldn't end up like—*Damn it*, Elle, I—" He turned away again and his shoulders rose. Then he strode back toward the stairs to the top deck.

"I did not write that note only because I thought you wished to make atonement," she said to his back.

"Is that so?" he said diffidently, mounting the steps.

"I was frightened." She scrambled up after him. The breeze buffeted her hair and gown and she exclaimed, "I *am* frightened. I have never known a man like you. I have never known a man so thoroughly good-hearted. I thought—I don't know what I thought but I'm frightened."

He turned to her, but he said nothing.

Her throat was closing up. "You wrote to Lady Justice."

He frowned. "How do you—"

"She demanded that Mr. Brittle forgive me for the missing type. She said if he did not do so, and increase my wages, that she would go to another printer."

His face was a mélange of relief and pleasure and pain. "Fine then," he said only. "Fine."

"You *wrote* to her."

He shrugged and looked over her head and his blue, blue eyes studied the complex crisscrossing of masts and ropes and furled sails, assessing carefully. "Surprised she even got the gist of it," he said. "Disaster of a scrawl. I'm not that hawk fellow you want."

"Ain't."

"What's that?"

"You *ain't* that hawk fellow."

"Gabrielle." His voice was abruptly tight.

"Anthony."

"*Don't.*" He ran his hand over his face. Dropping his gaze, he stared fixedly at the deck before his boots. "Temper's not what it—what it should be at present. Not suitable for feminine company."

"Forgive me, Anthony. I am sorry."

"I am too. Thought I'd—" He bit back his speech.

"You thought what?"

He met her gaze directly. "I thought I'd found you."

"Found me?" she whispered.

"The one. The perfect woman for me. The only woman. That day, with your grandmother, I looked at her and saw what you'd become someday."

"Poor, blind, and ill?"

He smiled gently. "Beautiful. As you are now. Forty, fifty years from now, still beautiful. Your eyes, your smile. I saw myself all those years in the future, holding that woman's hand and loving her as much as I do now. More, daresay." He drew a deep breath. "But I'm not the man you want, Elle. I can't write a clever letter. I can't even write a clever word. And I can't pretend that I don't love you when I do. That ain't me." His eyes jerked upward. "*Isn't.*"

"I don't want him. I never wanted him. I wanted them."

"Them?"

"Lady Justice and Peregrine. Them together. How they cannot seem to get enough of each other, even when they are at each other's throats for all the world to see. Their spark. Their devotion to each other. I want that."

"You want that?"

"I want *you*. Because I feel that way with you. I have felt it since you walked into the shop and made me drink ale, and every moment since. I feel so alive with you, so happy. You make me laugh and you make me hum when I don't even know I'm humming and you make me want to speak with contractions and strip off every piece of clothing and throw myself at you. You make me feel everything I thought I would never be allowed to feel. I love you, Anthony."

A burst of air escaped his lungs and his eyes were bright.

"Please accept me, Captain," she said, "even though I am a scoundrel."

In an instant she was in his arms and her mouth was beneath his. They kissed and she sighed and he held her close and it didn't matter that all the world could see. He was hers and he was wonderful.

"We've a bit of a problem, Elle," he said, nuzzling her throat and then the edge of her lips.

"*We.* I like that," she murmured. "But what problem could we possibly have?"

"Just signed on again." He kissed her. "Admiralty's thrilled." He kissed her again. "Gave me command of this first-rate beauty, *Princess Donna.* Sparkling new, just launched out of dry dock. Forty-eight guns."

"How splendid! Congratulations." She smiled up at him. "I will miss you dreadfully. How long will you be away? A month? Two?"

"Two years."

Her eyes popped wide.

"Your good-bye note was very effective," he said.

"I don't suppose you can tell them you made a mistake?"

"I signed on with one condition. Told them there was a particular printing press maker in Philadelphia I'd like to visit. New platen design. Everybody's clamoring for it."

"You researched printing presses?"

"Thought I'd nab one for you. If you hadn't tied the knot with anybody else by then, I hoped I might be able to entice you with it."

"Are you telling me that you rejoined the navy so that you could sail across the ocean, purchase a printing press, sail back to England with it, and use it to court me?"

"That's about the size of it."

"I love you, Anthony Masinter."

He kissed her yet again.

"Thing of it is," he murmured against her lips, "as captain I've the liberty to keep a wife aboard." He drew away to look into her eyes. "What say you, little print mistress?" The blue shone. "Care to join me at the altar before I'm obliged to cast off?"

"Yes. Oh, yes." She went onto her toes, pulled him down to her, and kissed him with every bit of happiness in her heart. He wrapped his hands around her face and for several sweet, delectable minutes made her very glad that she had reconsidered her notions about sailors.

"Will Lady Justice approve?" He stroked her cheek. "I hear she's none too keen on marriage."

"She isn't." She smiled into his loving eyes. "But she has never met my scoundrel."

A SELECTION OF LETTERS
and
Other Writings

BY

LADY JUSTICE
Advocate for All Britons

&

(Her Detractor and Nemesis)

PEREGRINE
Secretary, The Falcon Club

~

Presented to
His Majesty GEORGE IV
by
Captain Anthony Tallis Masinter
of the Royal Navy,
Upon the occasion of the birth of his daughter.

~

Selected & Edited
by
Gabrielle Elizabeth Masinter

SCOUNDREL PUBLISHING CO.
LONDON, ENGLAND
JULY 1822

Fellow Subjects of Britain,

How delinquent is Government if it distributes the sorely depleted Treasury of our Noble Kingdom hither and yon without recourse to prudence, justice, or reason?

Gravely so.

Irresponsibly so.

Villainously so!

As you know, I have made it my crusade to make public all such spendthrift waste. This month I offer yet another example: 14½ Dover Street.

What use has Society of an exclusive gentlemen's club if no gentlemen are ever seen to pass through its door? — that white-painted panel graced with an intimidating knocker, a Bird of Prey. But the door never opens. Do the exalted members of this club ever use their fashionable clubhouse?

It appears not.

Information has recently come to me through perilous channels I swim for your benefit, Fellow Subjects. It appears that without proper debate Lords has approved by Secret Ballot an allotment to the Home Office designated for this so-called club. And yet for what purpose does the club exist but to pamper the indolent rich for whom such establishments are already Legion? There can be no good in this Rash Expenditure.

I vow to uncover this concealed squandering of our kingdom's Wealth. I will discover the names of each member of this club, and the business or play that passes behind its imposing knocker. Then, dear readers, I will reveal it to you.

— Lady Justice

~o0o~

Fellow Britons,

I vowed I would not relent in my pursuit of information concerning the exclusive gentlemen's club at #14½ Dover

Street. I have not. I am now in possession of a curious fact. It is called The Falcon Club. Its members go by the names of birds. I haven't any idea the reason for this, but when I know I will tell you.

It would be wonderful if I discovered them to be a society of bird-watching experts. I might even join them if I could spare the time. But I doubt I will find that. Bird-watchers are quiet folk, but not to my knowledge particularly secretive.

— Lady Justice

~o0o~

Fellow Britons,

I recently received the following communication through my publisher:

> *Dear Lady Justice,*
> *Your impertinence astounds me. But your tenacity must be commended. I fear I have already, in fact, come to admire you for that. But, dear lady, if you wish admittance to the Falcon Club so desperately, you have only to discover the names of its members and apply to join. One, I regret to report, has recently left us. But four of us remain. Among these is myself,*
>
> *Your servant,*
> *Peregrine*
> *Secretary, The Falcon Club*

Impertinence, indeed. This Peregrine seeks to intimidate me with soft words and flatteries, common methods by which the powerful and wealthy cajole and control society. Rest assured, my head will not be turned. I shall continue to seek out wasteful expenditures of funds and lay them open to examination before the entire kingdom.

— Lady Justice

~o0o~

Fellow Britons,

The people of our great kingdom must not see another farthing of their livelihoods squandered on the idle rich. Thus, my quest continues! In rooting out information concerning that mysterious gentleman's establishment at 14 ½ Dover Street, the so-called Falcon Club, I have learned an intriguing morsel of information. One of its members is a sailor and they call him Sea Hawk.

Birds, birds and more birds! Who will it be next, Mother Goose?

Unfortunately I have not learned the name of his vessel. But would it not be unsurprising to discover him to be a member of our Navy or a commissioned privateer? Yet another expenditure of public funds on the personal interests of those whose privilege is already mammoth.

I will not rest until all members of the Falcon Club are revealed or, due to my investigating, the club itself disbands in fear of thorough detection.

— Lady Justice

~o0o~

Madam,

Your persistence in seeking the identities of the members of our humble club cannot but gratify. How splendid for us to claim the marked attentions of a lady of such enterprise.

You have hit the mark. One of us is indeed a sailor. I wish you the best of good fortune in determining which of the legion of Englishmen upon the seas he is. But wait! May I assist? I am in possession of a modest skiff. I shall happily lend it to you so that you may put to sea in search of your quarry. Better yet, I shall work the oars. Perhaps sitting opposite as you peer over the foamy swells I will find myself as enamored of your beauty as I am of your tenacious intelligence—for only a beauty would hide behind such a daunting name and project.

I confess myself curious beyond endurance, on the verge of seeking your identity as assiduously as you seek ours. Say the word, madam, and I shall have my boat at your dock this instant.

Yours,
Peregrine
Secretary, The Falcon Club

~o0o~

Odwall Blankton Fishery, Billingsgate Wharf
RECEIPT OF PURCHASE:
10 lbs Mackerel, Smoked
20 lbs Sole
1 doz. Lobsters, live
2 lbs Sturgeon Roe
3 doz. Oysters
20 Lemons
TO BE DELIVERED TO: Lady Justice, Brittle & Sons, Printers, London
ATTACHED: My lady, with my compliments. Peregrine

~o0o~

Fellow Subjects of Britain,

The arrogance of the aristocracy never ceases to amaze. Consider the following, which I received yesterday from the Head Bird Man:

My Lady,

It is with great pleasure that I alert you to the news that Sea Hawk has returned to England and is forthwith available for you to run to ground. I fear that once you become acquainted with him you will have no use for the remaining members of our inconsequential little club; he tends to turn ladies' heads. If this comes to pass, my heart will suffer for loss of your attention.

But I cannot regret that finally you may discover the identity of one of us. Therefore, if you should in fact learn his true name, pray do me the honor of conveying to me your meeting place and time so that I might hide in the bushes and sigh over the loss I am myself now bringing about. A lady must be given that which she wishes, however, and if I am able to fulfill your desires even in this manner I will eagerly do so, even though it is to my disadvantage.

Yours devotedly, &c,

Peregrine

Secretary, The Falcon Club

He teases as though I were a demi-rep he might charm with childish flattery. He imagines women bereft of the capacity to reason, susceptible to empty foolishness instead.

Note this, Peregrine: I am unmoved by your flirtation. I will discover Sea Hawk's true identity and will reveal him and all of you to the poor citizens of Britain whose wealth you squander playing games like little boys at pick-up-sticks.

— Lady Justice

~o0o~

Dearest Lady,

I give to you now only that which any gentleman admirer might give to a lady: poetry. Samuel Taylor Coleridge, to be precise. I offer it because having received back all the gifts I have sent to you, I need guidance as to what you may accept from me as gift. Quoth the Ancient Mariner:

> "If he may know which way to go;
> For she guides him smooth or grim.
> See, brother, see! how graciously
> She looketh down on him."

My lady, looketh down on me with gracious mercy and

return not this humble gift.

Yours &c,
Peregrine
Secretary, The Falcon Club

  * Editor's Note: Among these gifts delivered to Brittle & Sons, Printers, was a life-sized statue of a mermaid. —G.M.

~o0o~

Peregrine,

  You preen. You strut. You will be plucked. Then I will have only this to say to you, "The game is done! I've won! I've won!"

— Lady Justice

  * Editor's Note: Here Lady Justice also quotes from Coleridge's *Rhyme of the Ancient Mariner*. —G.M.

~o0o~

My Dearest Lady,

  I write with unhappy news: Sea Hawk has quit the club. Thus our numbers are once more diminished. We are now a sorry small lot — only three. If you could see your way to resting your campaign against our poor little band of companions, I would nevertheless eternally count you the most worthy adversary and continue to sing your praises to all.
  I admit, however, that should you do so, I shall regret the loss of you.

Yours &c.
Peregrine
Secretary, The Falcon Club

~o0o~

To Peregrine:

Your cajoling fails to touch me. I will not rest. Be you three, two, or only one, I will find you and reveal you to public scrutiny. Take care, Mr. Secretary. Your day of reckoning will soon be at hand.

— Lady Justice

P.S. Thank you for the salted herring. You ought to have begun with that. I simply adore salted herring. You cretin.

~o0o~

Dear Lady Who Calls Herself Just,

I have waited these months for news that would assure me of your continued interest in my club. Alas, none has come. Your latest publications say nothing of our humble band of friends. I grow uneasy that you have relinquished your project of uncovering us, and I find myself jealous of the regular subjects of your pamphlets. How can those unfortunates claim your attention when I cannot? And how unjust you are to have forgotten my friends and me, when you had promised to pursue us. Can your character be so inconstant? I will not believe it!

Continually yours,
Peregrine
Secretary, The Falcon Club

~o0o~

To Peregrine, at large:

Rather than my character, your intelligence is inconstant, or indeed non-existent. And how like an aristocrat to believe you deserve attention above all others. Yes, wounded veterans of war, orphans, chimney sweeps, and stevedores interest me more than your elite cabal. Yes, their struggles to provide for their families concern me more greatly than the waste of Government funds on your little club. Yes, I would rather think and write about them than about you and your pampered friends.

You see, I care for these people—deeply, honestly, in my heart. Unlike you, they are not garbed in costly raiment, they do not sit languidly sipping imported spirits while others rush about serving them, and they do not reside in vast mansions or gather with their friends at fashionable venues. They are poor, struggling, and overburdened with the labor that underpins this kingdom. They need me. You do not, except to expose you to the Good People of this Nation as villainous parasites.

I have not ceased my pursuit of you. I simply have others who interest me more.

— Lady Justice

~o0o~

Dear Lady,

Extraordinary! If I make myself desperate and destitute, will it inspire your continued interest? Shall I tear off my fine garments and cast away my wealth in order to ensure your devoted attention? Can this be the sort of man you admire?

Incredulously yours,
Peregrine
Secretary, The Falcon Club

~o0o~

To Peregrine, at large:

Yes. I dare you.

— Lady Justice

~o0o~

Dear Lady,

It is done—the moment you throw off the mask behind which you hide. Do so, and I will surrender.

Yours,
Peregrine
Secretary, The Falcon Club

~o0o~

Fellow Subjects of Britain,

Scandal!

At night I lie abed, heart pounding, breaths short, and mourn England's ravagement. My soul cries and my frail feminine form aches to know that the Elite of Society to whom we all pay homage are stealing from our Kingdom to serve their profligate ways.

Stealing!

For four years now I have sought the identities of the members of the elusive Falcon Club, a gentleman's leisure establishment that regularly receives funds from the Treasury without due process in Parliament. Today I announce my greatest accomplishment in this quest: I have discovered the identity of one member. I have hired an assistant to follow this man and learn of his activities. When I possess reports that I can trust, I will convey them to you.

Until then, if you are reading this pamphlet, Mr. Peregrine, know that I look forward to the day you and I meet face-to-face and I will tell you exactly what sort of man you truly are.

—Lady Justice

~o0o~

My Dearest Lady,

I am nearly breathless (as I daresay three-quarters of the

men in London are now) imagining you at rest upon your cot, your breast filled with emotion, your lips trembling with feeling. I am moved by your devotion. And, like a cock released into the ring, I am roused by your eagerness to meet me in person.

But perhaps you have discovered not one of my fellow club members, but me. Perhaps I shan't be obliged to wait long for us to finally become acquainted. Perhaps my own nocturnal imaginings will soon rush from the realm of dreams into reality. I can only hope.

Increasingly yours,
Peregrine
Secretary, the Falcon Club

~o0o~

Fellow Subjects,

I have frustrating news. The man I hired to follow the member of the Falcon Club that I discovered has lost the trail. I share with you this information because I have had letters from many of you excited at my discovery, and I cannot bear to hold you in suspense. It warms my heart that you are as desirous as I to know the truth of this club.

—Lady Justice

~o0o~

Dearest Lady,

I beg of you—mercy! You must cease this teasing prose. When you write of warmth, your heart, and desire all in the same sentence, I vow I can barely hold my seat. I would erect a tent before the office of your publisher and sleep in it nights in the hopes of capturing a glimpse of you entering the building upon the dawn. Indeed, I have attempted it! Alas, the street warden will not allow it. Thus I am forced to beg of you, my lady, consider my febrile imagination and give it rest.

Increasingly yours, &c.,

Peregrine

Secretary, The Falcon Club

~oOo~

Fellow Subjects of Britain,

Due to Unanticipated Circumstances my agent in Shropshire is once again detained in pursuing his Falcon Club quarry. In short, I begin to despair of this particular quest.

No—I shan't cease seeking justice! Yes—I shall hound the members of this wasteful club until they are all discovered!

But, as I have fretfully awaited my agent's communications, I have learned a valuable lesson: subterfuge is not my bailiwick. I would rather approach a man directly, accuse him of wrongdoing justifiably and without recourse to secrecy, and hear him defend himself with mine own ears than sit like an Eastern despot upon his throne who waits for his henchmen to perform Despicable Deeds in his name. My methods must remain pristine so that my victory is too.

I have not recalled my agent from the countryside; his troubles are sufficiently noisome to inhibit his progress without my intervention. But when he is again mobile I will inform him of my desire to quit this project. For now. For when this Falcon Club member returns to London, I will confront him and he will be obliged to answer to you, the People of Britain, for his criminal excess.

—Lady Justice

~oOo~

My Dearest lady,

I breathe a sigh of profound relief. Quit your pursuit of my fellow club member, indeed. But know this: I am already in

London. I entreat you, pursue me instead. If you should find
me, I promise you a most satisfying Interrogation.

In eager anticipation,
Peregrine
Secretary, The Falcon Club

~o0o~

My Dearest Lady Justice,

My admiration for you has grown such that I cannot hide
the news: I have lost another member of the Falcon Club.
Since you have become so adept at hounding down my fellow
club members, I wonder if I could prevail upon you to search
out this one and bring her back into the fold. She is difficult to
miss: walks with a stoop, carries a cane, suffers from myopia. I
haven't an idea as to where she has gone. Perhaps your
sleuthing skills will save the day.

With all my gratitude and ever increasing affection,
Peregrine
Secretary, The Falcon Club

~o0o~

To Peregrine, at large:

You are a cabbage head. I hadn't any idea that one of your
members was a lady. I am not a nitwit, Mr. Bird Man. You
chose to describe a woman of ill appearance to make my quest
seem ridiculous. But your attempt at cleverness reveals you;
you would not have mentioned a lady at all if there weren't one
in your club. No gentleman would have even paused to
consider it.

Point goes to Lady Justice.

You are arrogant and bored, and thus seek to taunt me to
amuse yourself. Idle wealth corrupts as swiftly as absolute
power. You, Mr. Peregrine, are corrupted.

— Lady Justice

~oOo~

My Dearest Lady,

To be corrupted with you would be to live heaven upon earth. Name the day, the hour, the location. I will bring a single red rose and my ardor.

Yours entirely,
Peregrine

~oOo~

My Fellow Subjects of Britain,

The King is dead. Long live the King. And, apparently, his coronation crown. My sources within St James's Palace tell me that our august new monarch is so enamored of the crown constructed for his coronation ceremony that he has petitioned Government to purchase it outright. An elaborate collection of silver, gold and diamonds that graced His Majesty's brow for only a few fleeting moments, it cost the Treasury of this Kingdom more than twenty-five thousand pounds to hire the jewels for the occasion. Now he wishes to further deplete the Royal Coffers so that he can, every morning when waking and every evening when retiring, feast his eyes upon its magnificence and in doing so know himself to be worthy of the honor of his God-given place.

I am nearly speechless. Members of Parliament, if you approve this expenditure, the People of this Nation will finally know you entirely bereft of wisdom and restraint, and rise up in protest. Allow good sense to guide you. Dismantle the coronation crown before it dismantles our kingdom.

— Lady Justice

~oOo~

My Lady,

It seems from your latest incitation to revolution that you actually glimpsed the coronation crown. You must have been in the crowd at the festivities. Did my gaze traveling over the press of people rest upon your face without knowing you? What a tragedy, that I might have seen you and failed to recognize in your eyes that glimmer of rebellion that is spectacularly, uniquely yours.

But could I have in fact seen you? For on that day as I looked about the place I vow that I felt a frisson of awareness pass through me, a thrilling shock of sensation that I can only call the heat of intimate familiarity. Was I perhaps at that moment looking upon you? I would be wrong to doubt it. For any man knows that the ignorant eye sometimes does not clearly see what the heart recognizes well.

> With new hope,
> Peregrine
> Secretary, The Falcon Club

~o0o~

To Peregrine, at large:

As always the evidence upon which you base your conclusions is faulty. You assume that I attended the festivities only because I wrote a meager description of the crown that I might have overheard anywhere in London. Even had I attended the event, how do you imagine my face would be one you chose to look upon? Perhaps I was among the people pressing at the barriers along the route but shut out of the sacred ceremony itself. Then you would not have seen me, would you? For you have no interest in such people. If you ever even look upon the faces of your own servants, I would be astonished.

You are nonsensical and lost in adolescent fantasies. Are you a Man or, as I have often wondered, merely a Boy?

— Lady Justice

~oOo~

Dear Treasured Lady,

That you have wondered about me gives me every kind of hope. As for my manhood, you question it so often that I am beginning to suspect you would like to see it.

Somewhat breathlessly,
Peregrine
Secretary, The Falcon Club

~oOo~

Fellow Subjects of Britain,

While many of you have written begging me to publish that conceited aristocrat's latest letter, I cannot satisfy you. With it he has descended into puerile taunt, and I publish only that which I hope will edify.

As to you, Mr. Peregrine, I will not blush, stammer, or shrink away from your teasing. I am no fragile flower to wilt over a salacious suggestion, rather the opposite. I am stronger than your wildest dreams.

I say to you, Mr. Secretary: bring it on.

— Lady Justice

~oOo~

Lady Justice,

You speak of my dreams. Know you, then, how often you appear in them? Take care, dear lady, for you are in danger of making me even more thoroughly your devoted servant.

Faithfully,
Peregrine

Secretary, The Falcon Club

~o0o~

Dearest Lady (without whose attention I languish, and without whose sweet condemnations—offered so generously—I would barely know myself a Cretin and instead be called, mistakenly, Man),

I write to you in dismay, for I have received news of a Most Distressing Nature: The last remaining member of my club is to marry. When marry, how, and to whom, I will leave to your journalistic perspicacity. Know only this, that in anticipation of the event I am bereft. For upon that day when bells chime in the church tower to announce the vows are said, I will be left alone. The Falcon Club that was once five will be only one in number: me.

And so I write to you with this plea: Do not abandon me as my companions have. Remain with me (in such a manner as you have allowed this concourse betwixt us), give me your counsel (as you are ever eager to do) to relieve my dejection, your wisdom (immense, quick, and astonishing) to calm my lonesome fidgets, and your bosom (metaphorically, of course) as a cushion for my cheek when I need the most simple comfort—the comfort of knowing that I am yet in the mind and heart of one inestimable Friend.

I claim this succor of you knowing that your generosity in giving it will only confirm in my breast that Profound Admiration that I have had for you these five years of our correspondence.

Ever Yours,
Peregrine
Secretary, The Falcon Club

~o0o~

To Peregrine, at large:

My cheeks are free of tears for you. No man who deserves friends has cause to fear their loss. Moping is the privilege of the pampered classes. Boredom that you inflict upon yourself is your true enemy. I recommend that you find some useful employment worthy of a Man rather than a Mobcap.

— Lady Justice

~o0o~

Dearest Lady,

I will make my case more plainly to you: I have lost my friends. Each of them, one at a time, has fallen into Hymen's choking snare, and I mourn for them as well as for my loss of them. For marriage—as you, a lady of Violent Independence, must agree—is but a prison to subjugate both body and will to the whims of another. Woe to the ensnared whose betrothed in courtship is all charm, laughter, and generosity of spirit, but who after the vows are exchanged is revealed to be capricious, vain, and greedy for attention.

We all know, of course, that this is more common than not.

With great respect,
Peregrine
Secretary, The Falcon Club

~o0o~

To Peregrine, at large:

You have lost your senses, even those few that you might have previously possessed. That said, at long last I find myself in agreement with you on one matter: marriage is a prison. But not for men. The Law does not bind husbands; rather, wives. Even the sacred vows instruct a woman to love, cherish, and obey while a man must only love and cherish. Why must a wife promise to obey when a husband must not?

Therefore, as ever, I am unimpressed with your woe.

— Lady Justice

~oOo~

Dearest Lady,

You claim that a husband's marriage vows promise less than a wife's. And yet here is his vow: "With this ring I thee wed, with my body I thee worship, and with all my worldly goods, I thee endow." That is, he gives her everything he has. He worships her like a goddess.

What more, kind lady, can you expect a man to give?

In long-suffering affection,
Peregrine
Secretary, The Falcon Club

~oOo~

To Peregrine, at large:

No doubt it has escaped your notice from your height of privilege that—despite the sacred words that you quote—when a woman weds, the Law of this Kingdom places her income, belongings, indeed her entire person in the possession of her husband. She has no power or authority over her money, her property, her children, even her own body. She can do nothing without his consent, including leave him if he treats her with cruelty.

Marriage does not bestow upon a woman a devotee. It shackles her to a prison guard.

— Lady Justice

~oOo~

Dear Lady,

I understand. You do not like marriage. Neither do I. From whichever direction one looks at it, it is a trap.

But, if you will, consider the principal benefit of the wedded state, which I cannot give a name to here (out of deference to your modesty), but which, assured every night, must be an advantage to both husband and wife. In rejecting marriage, are you so willing to relinquish that as well?

In doubt, yet most sincerely,
Peregrine
Secretary, The Falcon Club

~o0o~

To Peregrine, at large:

You seek to shock, or perhaps to titillate. You do neither. What antiquated, patriarchal notion of femininity suggests to you that a woman must first bind herself in marriage to enjoy that benefit which is readily available outside of the wedded state?

— Lady Justice

~o0o~

Dear Lady,

I can hardly write. My hand quivers so that the ink from my pen splatters on the page and I find myself obliged to blot it again and again.

I renew to you now my invitation to meet. Any time. Any place.

With hope,
Peregrine
Secretary, The Falcon Club

~o0o~

To Peregrine, at large:

In response to the invitation in your last letter, I offer three words: in your dreams.

— Lady Justice

~o0o~

Dear Lady Justice,

In sorrow I write to you a final time. The Falcon Club is no more. I beg of you, do not weep for this loss too bitterly. You have other poor souls to badger and other unworthy causes to pursue for the entertainment of your readers. Know, however, that my days will be duller, my nights meaningless, without your correspondence to sustain me. Only, dear lady, do not forget me. For I will most certainly not forget you.

With eternal admiration,
Peregrine
No longer Secretary, The Falcon Club

* Editor's Note: Although Lady Justice continues to write publicly to the People and Rulers of Great Britain, she has not again mentioned Peregrine in the months since their last exchange. It is this editor's fondest hope that they have finally met face-to-face, and that they have reconciled their differences sufficient to find pleasure in each other at long last. —G.M.

THE EARL

*How does a bookish lady bring an arrogant lord to his knees?
Entice him to Scotland, strip him of titles and riches, and make
him prove what sort of man he truly is.*

Opposites...

Handsome, wealthy, and sublimely confident, Colin
Gray, the new Earl of Egremoor, has vowed to unmask the
rabble-rousing pamphleteer, Lady Justice, the thorn in
England's paw. And he'll stop at nothing.

Attract.

Smart, big-hearted, and passionately dedicated to her
work, Lady Justice longs to teach her nemesis a lesson in
humility. But her sister is missing, and a perilous journey with
her archrival across Scotland just might turn fierce enemies
into lovers.

~o0o~

Turn the page for preview of Lady Justice and Peregrine's
powerfully romantic love story...

Excerpt from The Earl

The moon had ceded the night to the stars when she arrived at the meeting place they had agreed upon via letter: a small ancient cemetery surrounded by a fence and hedges on a street still busy with carriages and horse traffic. A long black cloak and veil aided the dark in disguising her.

Jonah walked beside her, a hood drawn around his face as well, but he would not accompany her to the meeting. For all his taunting, Peregrine did not frighten her. A man who dedicated his leisure time to rescuing strays was unlikely to harm a lone woman.

The cobbles shimmered with an earlier rain as she gestured for Jonah to remain across the street. Lamps lit this part of London irregularly, and the break in the wall was in shadow. Beside the gate stood an enormous man.

"Ma'am." The behemoth bowed. "He awaits you within."

It was immediately clear why he had suggested this place. The thick hedge within the walls created a bower of privacy and the gravestones scattered unevenly throughout made swift escape impossible.

He had staged the situation to his advantage too. He stood among the stones not four yards away, a lamp on the ground behind him casting him in silhouette. He was tall, and the breadth of his shoulders and solid stance suggested a man of fine physical conditioning. The night was mild and he wore no hat or overcoat—nothing to disguise him.

He was entirely willing for her to know his true identity.

The gate creaked closed behind her.

"Good evening, madam," he said into the darkness. "It is a pleasure to finally make your acquaintance. I have looked forward to this moment for years. But, of course, you already know that." His voice was smooth and low, far from menacing, rather intimate, and shockingly, unbelievably, horribly familiar.

Only hours earlier this elegant voice had proposed marriage to her.

"I am Gray," he said. "Now remove that veil and tell me your name."

The Earl is available in ebook or paperback at booksellers everywhere.

To My Wonderful Readers

Many of you will have recognized in this novella my humble nod to *My Fair Lady*, one of my favorite musicals. While I was writing the ball scene in *The Scoundrel & I*, I went around the house singing, "I can tell that she was born Hungarian! Not only Hungarian, but of royal blood. She is a princess!" I simply could not resist the allusion. It was also my secret way of attaching this story to my novel *How to Be a Proper Lady*, which features sailors and includes a cameo of Bishop Frederick Baldwin. Two of my other seafaring heroes appear by name in this novella as well, Nik Acton of *A Lady's Wish* and Luc Westfall of *I Married the Duke*. For more of Tony, you can find him featured in my Prince Catchers Series novella, *Kisses, She Wrote*, which tells the story of Cam and Jacqueline's romance, and the prequel to that, *I Married the Duke*.

The Scoundrel & I is itself a prequel to *The Earl*, Lady Justice and Peregrine's love story and the finale to my Falcon Club Series (published by Avon Books). Of their letters collected at the end of this novella, many are drawn from the first four books in the series: *When a Scot Loves a Lady, How to Be a Proper Lady, How a Lady Weds a Rogue*, and *The Rogue*. (*The Rogue* double-duties as the first book in my Devil's Duke Series). You can find plenteous information about all my series and books on my website at www.KatharineAshe.com. While you're there, I hope you will subscribe to my e-mailing list to receive announcements about my new books as well as a free Falcon Club short story.

A final fun historical note: in the final chapter of *The Scoundrel & I*, I included *Falconer's New Universal Dictionary of the Marine* as a nod to my Falcon Club Series. But it was indeed a real reference book originally published in 1769, and almost entirely revised for the second edition in 1815. It is a big, thick, wonderful compendium of all things nautical and it plays a key role in my novel *In the Arms of a Marquess*.

Thank You!

The help of generous friends and colleagues made this book possible. Thank you to Marcia Abercrombie, Georgie C. Brophy, Nita Eyster, Sonja Foust, Lee Galbreath, Meg Huliston, Beverly Jenkins, Caroline Linden, Mary Brophy Marcus, Stephanie McCullough, Miranda Neville (especially for Lady Gaga), Maya Rodale, and Jen Underhill, and special thanks to Diane Michel (for hatching bridges). To Donna Finlay, whose kind query regarding Lady Justice and Peregrine's letters inspired this entire book, and for her generosity of spirit, I am especially grateful. To all of my Princesses, who have helped me with many details of this book and others, I dedicate it with profound and affectionate gratitude.

Copious thanks to the talented women whose work is all over this book: Georgann T. Brophy, Lori Devoti, Carrie Divine, my editor Anne Forlines, and copy editor Martha Trachtenberg. To Cari Gunsallus, the most wonderful author's assistant in the world, and to Kimberly Whalen, my fabulously supportive agent, I send up special thanks.

I am so grateful for my precious writing companion, Idaho, and for my husband and son whose constant and loving support and enthusiasm are the wind in my sails.

Last but never least, to my readers whose letters, emails, tweets, and posts mean more than you can know, from the bottom of my heart I thank you.